A SOCIABLY AWKWARD (FRYING) PAN

The Holloway Years

An Autobiographical Psychological Humorous Greek Cypriot Tragedy

By Panico Antoniou

* * *

An autobiography of an ordinary man who achieves nothing notable in life against a challenging upbringing

* * *

A sequel to the yet to be written best seller
The Cyprus Years....

* * *

Now with a social media accompaniment....
Search "Sociably Awkward Frying Pan" on Facebook.

* * *

I would like to thank "My-Annie" for helping me along the way in achieving my dream. I would like to thank my children for making it easy for me to reach that dream. You guys are all that I ever wanted, all that I ever hoped to achieve and be. Only you guys can tell me if I succeeded.........

... I am being a soppy-sod!
Apparently all "authors" do this....

The Holloway Years, By Panico Antoniou

Cover designed by Frying Pan

This book is not a work of fiction. Names, characters, places, and incidents are products of the author's memories. Any resemblance to other actual persons, living or dead, events, or locales is entirely coincidental in a spooky doppelganger sort of way.

Author Panico Antoniou
Visit me on Facebook -Sociably Awkward Frying Pan
Feel free to email the author at panico.antoniou@btinternet.com

Printed in the United Kingdom near the Holloway Road

First Printing: April 2018

CONTENTS

PREFACE:- SOCIABLY VERSES SOCIALLY

So here it is. My finished autobiography.
I feel that I should greet you in the manor my father used to greet rich diners at his restaurant – in that Basil Fawlty, over exuberant clumsy way during Basil's Gourmet Night.
Then again, I don't want to come across as an arse-licker. Not that my father was an arse-licker. He felt flattered – as I am now.
I am humbled that you have purchased an autobiography of an average working class bloke who has lived (*thus far) an unremarkable life.
*thus far – with regards to that I am still living and not that I expect or should wish that my life was anything but unremarkable. Then again...it depends on how people judge an unremarkable life. All it takes is for one person to make a remark on one's life and that life ceases to be unremarkable!

So thanks again for reading this and hope you enjoy some of the following chapters.
Oh - I've got to be honest. Some early chapters make pretty poor reading....but then later on, there is a marked improvement as I get the hang of this writing malarkey!

This book isn't going to make the Amazon best-selling autobiographies list... but since you are stuck with it – give it a go... If anything...you can stick two fingers up to the "literary

establishment" by supporting self-publishers to get their stories out in their own words.
Hark at me getting all militant.

This is the last chapter to be written and I am required to add this quick explanation as to why I used "*Sociably Awkward*" instead of "*Socially Awkward*" in the title of my autobiography. You may also ask why the last chapter to be written is inserted at the beginning and the reason is that, had I not, my proof readers (my two daughters) would have refused to proof-read and go on strike. It's a disclaimer!

As it happens, I can get away with inserting this chapter here just by calling it – The Preface.
The insertion of this clarification is a negotiated compromise.
My daughters are insisting that I change the title from "A Sociably Awkward Frying Pan" to "A Socially" Awkward....."
They have said that people would be put off by the poor grammar on the title page.
I said - wait until they continue to read, then they will see poor grammar all right!
My son by the way wasn't that bothered as he is a teenager and nothing bothers him.

My kids grew up listening to my funny and quirky stories about my upbringing. I would tell them about my antics and hardships in order to....
(a) Inform them that life can be tough.
(b) Don't do as I say or do – or did.

(c) Some stories have messages – be they hidden and...
(d) Some are funny....well to me at least.
There is an (e) which is that my past may have a bearing as to why I am awkward in certain situations. Why I sometimes struggle. Why I can lose it and shrink into my shell.
Writing this is a way to inform my kids of what my wife realised early on in our marriage - I have a few issues!
How she stayed with me after thirty years I'll never know.

I am not a writer. I only got a Grade C in O-level English.
To me ***Socially Awkward*** means that I am not good in groups or that outside of work I am unsocial – which is not true as when conditions are right, I'm a barrel of laughs and when egged on, can be influenced into doing something totally stupid!
Sociably Awkward to me means that I express myself differently. I can be erratic and depressive and find it easy to separate myself from family and friends.
There are many times when I want to be alone and I will create distance between myself and those who class me as a friend. I can be rude and dismissive and I will always be suspicious of people's good intentions. I am paranoid and expect to be hurt one way or another. I hold grudges and I cannot forgive even the slightest transgression.
There is a flip side. My wife and kids are everything and I will do anything for them (within my ability and frame of mind). I am insular that way.

As Hugh Grant said in the film About A Boy – "*Every man is an island. And I stand by that. But clearly, some men are part of island chains*".

So – above is my dodgy explanation of why I have used Sociably Awkward.
Even though I'm wrong – I cannot change now.

The above is bullshit. It's just me - subconsciously non-conforming

………..

Psychology of oneself.
I've discovered this helps and thus can make an open and candid deduction.

EPIGRAPHS

"*I cannot think of any need in childhood as strong as the need for a father's protection*"
-Sigmund Freud

"*Carol? Who's Carol?*"
-Antonis

"*If you didn't have all that lipstick on, I would kiss you*"
-Panico Antoniou

Come Desdemona, Once more, well met at Cyprus.
-William Shakespeare's' Othello

INTRODUCTION I

Mountains were not climbed and disabilities were not overcome.....correction, physical disabilities were not overcome (not that I have any physical disabilities....unless you count chronic backache).
Mental disabilities remain to be seen.
Songs will not be written and no history books will contain my name or exploits.
Exploits is the wrong word. It implies that there could have been achievements but I am too modest to mention them, or that my achievements reached a level just below legend status. But there isn't anything like that here. Not unless you count street-legend status achieved by going round the neighbourhood armed with two ice-lolly sticks used as tongs, collecting dog poo in a crisp bag to use in a prank that literally backfired. See Chapter 11.

The writing will be awful and I'll be using a thesaurus for big words. I have no pre-plan layout and will be writing this on the hoof.
The story/autobiography will not flow and I may repeat or even forget where I am in the book.
I will not be using speech marks to the bewilderment of my proof readers –my two daughters.
The first draft did have speech marks, but it didn't look right – it looked like I was writing fiction.

These are my memories, my thoughts. I am not quoting anybody but only what my mind recollects of the events at that time. So grammatically the rules go out the window. However in order to compromise with my proof readers, I will use the Greek grammar symbols for quotations (even though they're not quotes) and speech text in italics.
For example, *<Pan, is that dog shit on your back...?>*
Just to add to the confusion, I will use inverted commas to indicate phrases or non-speech quotes. You'll see as you continue – IF you continue.
Girls – it's my book my rules.

I have a friend who, after watching the movie Gladiator (Russell Crowe not the Victor Mature one) inspired him to go and change his life. He learnt to say fuck-it and stopped taking shit. He got a new job, went travelling and stood up for himself in confrontations.
This book will not inspire you to do that!

Just googled – it's Ridley Scott's Gladiator.
I wasn't going to mention that I googled the director and was going to re-write the above with - *I had a friend who after watching the Ridley Scott's movie Gladiator...*but then changed my mind and not only did I not correct the above line to make me sound intelligent, but I left the action of "googling" so to emphasise the point that I am writing on the hoof. Personally, if any Ridley Scott movie was to change my early life, it would be The Martian. Man/boy on his own, growing potatoes in shit and enjoying the endless peace and sunsets.

According to Google, sunsets are blue on Mars and you have to wait forty minutes more to see a sunset on Mars compared to being on planet Earth.

Anyway - You will not be left on the edge of your seat.
You will not be educated (bar my odd Google moments and some insight into Cypriot culture), nor will you be left with that feeling that I too have to download and watch Gladiator.
What I can promise you is some sort of love, moderate violence, awkward near-sex ventures, mindless acts of petty vandalism and the image that when I was eleven, I found a Polaroid of my mother topless - that to this day has left me mentally scarred.

You're not in for a rollercoaster ride, but you will be left with one question and one critique.
How did this guy learn to read? Man his grammar is crap!
All told, one question and one criticism will be expected....or two 1 star ratings.
Actually, that's not correct. Everybody (that's all six of you who purchased or got a free copy) may mark it as 1 star.
If you are thinking of issuing me a single star....didn't you see my disclaimer?

I've jumped back to this introduction to add that I confuse there and their. I tend to use the wrong one in a line of text...anyway, I'm off back to Chapter 13 – subtitled -The first love of my life (I was sixteen and the barmaid was forty three).
You'll be better off going there via chapters 1-11.

CHAPTER 1:-IN THE BEGINNING, A BIT OF THE MIDDLE AND THE DAY OF MY DAD'S FUNERAL

I was born to Greek Cypriot parents who emigrated from Cyprus and to be honest, should not have been married in the first place. But a small dowry, coupled with the fact that they were the only young couple in the village educated to beyond a reading-capable level, resulted in a marriage of suitability and convenience.

I would imagine (but not too hard) that there was an element of lust and love that brought them together. Having five kids does tend to cement that view.

I don't want to sound dismissive of their relationship, but some people are better people when they are not married to each other for the promise of a Cypriot donkey and a cart with a dodgy wheel.

Yep, being a bit rude now. The dowry wasn't a donkey. It was probably a lace tablecloth and a fig tree or something like that.

They were tough times 1950s Cyprus. Poverty, intercommunal strife and second cousins marrying second cousins, so who am I to judge! My parents, by the way were not second cousins nor related till after their wedding.

An Indian friend of mine said their dowry consists of gold. Just thought I'd throw that in.

I've paused at this point................
It is early on in this book and I'm coming across as a total arsehole. I'm sounding cold and bitter. Do I / did I hate my parents? No way. I love/loved them both, but looking back at my childhood and how I am with my kids....... There is a slight envy. Not of my kids, just that feeling that things could have been easier, better for us kids back then, growing up with dysfunctional parents - but great individuals. Anyway, I will get to that later in later chapters...

Continue...
So to recap, my parents married, they were very poor and jobs in Cyprus were hard to come by.
Polaroid cameras were not invented!
On top of that, the grandmothers (my parents mothers) were going to kill each other with sticks at first and then with Cypriot worry-beads used as Bolas.
For those who can't be arsed to google Bolas, they're the type of slings with rock balls on the ends. You swing the Bolas above your head in an anticlockwise rotation and then release towards your target (in the Southern Hemisphere they swing them clockwise)!
It just occurred to me that you may not know what Cypriot worry-beads are. They are like pearls on a necklace, but made of wood or plastic, hence the Cypriots worry that they are not made of pearls.

When I was growing up, every Cypriot household had giant worry-beads hanging off walls and every uncle had a small set on his person. They would get them out (the worry-beads that is) and play with them by either counting each bead by pushing it around the loop or swinging the complete set around the back of your hand and back into your palm.
It was not uncommon for an old boy holding worry-Beads to count to many hundreds, even though the endless loop contained thirty beads.
Whenever a relative returned from a trip to Cyprus, they would bring you a set of worry-beads. We had a sideboard draw full of them. Sadly today, I don't know anybody who has a set, hence why the world has gone mad....with worry!

My dad made the decision to go to England in search of a better life and with the understanding that the British had forgotten our little independence skirmish.
I used the word "our" in the above sentence - as in "we Cypriots", but later on, I use "we" as in "we" English.
I do that when it suits. I sometimes use the "we" Greeks, especially when the Greece national football team won the Euros in 2004 (I think that was the year).
I won't google that, I'm on a roll here. We writers are like that!!

I need to make sure I get dates right because my dad left for England on his own without my mum. My elder brother and sister were born in Cyprus and then dad left.

I was the first of my clan to be born in Good Ole Blighty, (England) so you can see that any mistake in dates could lead to legal action, defamation of character and so on.
Now don't get me wrong and I am not having a cheap shot here, but my sister has blue eyes and blonde hair. Rare for Cypriots. Somewhere in chapter 9, I may mention the fights and name calling I use to aim at the milkman's daughter (insert smiley face).
And just in case I have sown seeds of doubt – my dad had fair hair and hazel eyes.
Me? I'm the darkest and shortest in the family!

Need to go a step back and mention the grandparents.
History has it that the grandmothers never got on. They were sworn enemies going back to the olive groves.
I met them once when I was sixteen.
Not sure if I should put this in its own chapter or continue. I may re-write and delete this.
---pause— yes I will leave the meeting of the grandmothers for later and insert the tale in its own chapter which for now let's call chapter X- Cyprus - the island of Aphrodite (writing on the hoof)!

By mentioning this now with the intention to tell the full story at a later chapter, it builds up some suspense and expectancy. Also, my first ever trip to Cyprus involves a trip to a prostitute and a meeting with the maternal grandfather (who just said, *so you're my grandson* and then walked away).
There was also the challenge of trying to shit through a hole in a wicker chair.

Bet you can't wait now.........

One grandparent I can mention in this chapter is my paternal grandfather. Sadly, he does not feature in the "Cyprus the island of Aphrodite" chapter because he passed away when my dad was young.
It was at four o'clock in the morning when my dad told me about the death of his father.
We closed the restaurant (to be mentioned in a coming chapter) and I was driving us home. I was tired and slightly over the alcohol limit.
I am sure today it's ok legally to say I was driving whilst pissed then, due the time that has elapsed.

(Just googled it and yep, I'm correct. Here in the UK it is called Limitation Period. I have also noticed on the same legal site that the Limitation Period for slander is one year. So, if I publish this book and do not promote for a whole year, some of the people mentioned in this book cannot sue).

My father was way over the limit. We were quarrelling whilst I was driving Airwolf – the name I gave my Ford Capri because of its sleek lines.
Airwolf was an early 80s TV series about a super helicopter. A cheaper version of the big budget Blue Thunder starring the guy who kills the shark in Jaws (*schmile you son of a bitch*).
As you can see, I'm done with fart-arsing about with google whist I've got the opposite of writer's cramp - wanker's wrist I think it's called.

So there we are having a bit of a slanging match. I can't remember what the argument was about, but I know I was very tired. The sun was coming up. The argument's getting heated and I was heading for a slap.
I pull the car over just in case the backhander puts me off my signalling, mirroring and manoeuvring. Or is it Mirror first?
I didn't have my full driving licence then, so it was very responsible and grown up of me to pull over. (Driving without a full licence – Limitation Period)!
The car is idling and Airwolf's arse is sticking out as I had yet to master the reverse park. I wound the window down for a quick getaway if things turned physical.
In those days, I mastered entering and exiting a car via the windows thanks to another TV show -The Dukes of Hazard. The car in that show had its doors welded shut and the redneck characters of the show would climb in and out of the car through the windows. Very cool!

The quarrel is in full swing, when unexpectedly there was a loud shriek which sounded like a crow squawking.
A recognisable sound if you ever watched the film The Omen.
You have now guessed that I was glued to the TV in those days.
My dad immediately stops shouting and sits there in contemplative silence (thanks thesaurus). I too stop and look at the old man.
To be honest, I'm thankful for the pause as things were getting out of hand and cutting remarks were flying from both sides.

If I felt uncomfortable, that was nothing compared to the look on my dad's face. He turns to me and proceeds to tell me about the day his father died.
It was the first time I heard this story.

My dad was twelve. He had left school by that age and was working in the local café making Greek coffee (far superior than Turkish coffee) for the hard-core coffee-drinking Backgammon playing locals.
Whilst my dad is serving the patrons sitting out in the middle of the village square, a bird (my dad believes to be a crow) lands on top of the café's stone building roof and starts squawking and has no intention of stopping.
The old boys stop slapping the Backgammon checkers and look up.
<Ahhh, N*ot a good sign*,> they all say in unison.
The old boys also comment on the fact that any bird flying around the village must be a wise old bird to avoid the lime covered sticks used to trap any local and migrating birds.

Cyprus is number one in the world for illegal bird trapping.
Campaigners say that a third of the world's migrating bird population never leaves Cyprus and ends up pickled.
Just google "Ambelopoulia" and you'll see what I mean.

Minutes later there was a big commotion and trucks can be seen speeding on gravel as dust fills the air.
Some of the workers from the nearby limestone quarry come to the square and one informs my dad and all the locals that

there was an accident and that his father (my grandfather) had died.
Turns out, the crow was a messenger, or as my dad believes (even on his death bed many years later) a visit from his dad taking one last look around.

I'm sat in Airwolf not knowing how to respond. I'm a cynic...I mean, I'm young, and what do I know about anything. I don't tell him that it was just a crow and it was coincidence that a bird is shrieking at the same time as he is informed of his father's tragic death. I don't tell him its mumbo-jumbo.
Did he think the crow we just heard was also a sign of some sort? Was this to be a life changing episode too? Was our argument going to get out of hand and did this crow bring him back from an action he'll regret later?
I just sit there and take in the show of emotion from a dad who in his (and my) early years, rarely interacted, except for disagreements, clashes and some very distressing episodes with my mum in the early hours keeping us youngsters awake with fear. Where was the crow then?
He continues to tell me about the hardships after his father's death and I sit there in silence.

There were times when I ashamedly and stupidly said that I hated him. But I knew then, as I know now that this wasn't the truth. Listening to him talking about his dad and how he supported his mother in Cyprus – I saw him in a different light.

I don't think that I will be able to explain my relationship with my dad or mum. I am hoping that this autobiography (which I wanted to write so that my kids could understand my quirks) might help me open up and perhaps get some answers myself. A journey of sorts....my Gladiator...Ridleys Scott's not Victor Mature's – which wasn't called Gladiator but Demetrius and The Gladiators!

I will write about my experiences and I will not judge.
Believe it or not, I felt that I had a great childhood. Crazy yes. Different, definitely, but I knew no better. Humor may have been a deciding factor which kept me partially glued together and then marrying "My Annie" stopped the spiral....but no doubt, it is the darker side of comedy which today I can relate too...

I need to quickly mention the day of my dad's funeral, then I can get on with telling you people about The Early Years – or as the sub-title is called –The Holloway years.
If I don't write a brief account of the events of that day now, then I will either make this self-published book twice as long in following chapters or heaven forbid write a sequel.
I did say that there would be no pre-plan laid out in this book and that I will jump from timeline to timeline, but hey, that's how my brain is working nowadays.

Today I am fifty-four years old. I married at twenty-four. From the day I married till three years before my dad's illness, we never saw each other and never spoke.

I was forty when my dad passed away.
My parents had divorced.
After I married, dad returned to Cyprus and opened a small garden centre and planted an olive grove.
At thirty-seven years of age, I had a yearning to see my dad, so out of the blue, during a holiday to Cyprus, I turned up on his doorstep with my wife and two daughters.
I approached his house alone. At first he did not recognise me and thought I was there to buy a fig-tree. Then he realised who I was and we coldly shook hands. He asked me if I was alone and I said no and that the wife and kids were in the car. I left them there just in case our meeting after all these years did not go well. I was wrong....we both were I guess.
He told me to go and fetch them. I called over to the girls and as they approached the house, my dad fell to his knees crying. I sometimes see the time before we met up again as time wasted. Then I think NO...this was the right time to meet up. I did not know what was around the corner. How would I feel now if he passed away before we made up?

We returned as a family the next year and for the first time ever, I felt a bond with a dad that I always wanted. Just a shame that it ruined my relationship with my mum who could not understand how I could make peace with a man that she (now I am struggling to find the right word because I don't think she loathed him) could not forgive.
Damned if I do and damned if I don't I guess.
And now, I have to find the *right time* all over again!

The final year, I returned to Cyprus without my wife and girls. I arrived with my older siblings. We got the news that my dad was terminally ill with cancer and he was given weeks to live. My younger siblings were just that...younger, a lot younger during those days of arguing and fighting and decided not travel to Cyprus. My logic is that (and I am no psychologist) there is a certain age where the mind can block out traumatic events with partial detriment or replace with dark humor. Then there is an age where the coping mechanism struggles. Yep – what utter bollocks I hear you say. But you know what??? Ridley Scott's Gladiator!
I'll try and make some sense of it later.....or you can come up with your own analysis.

The doctors were correct. It was only weeks. But I was not to know that doctors could be that accurate.
Upon seeing my father, I felt that they got the diagnosis wrong. This man isn't going to die. Not for a long time.
I told him that!
I stayed for a week and then I left to go back to England, with my older siblings agreeing to stay out there taking care of him. I was convinced he was not going to die. I promised him that I will return in a few months and he will be able to meet and spend time with his grandson.
...
I wasn't there when my dad died.
A day after I returned to England, I went back on line looking for the first (any) flight back out to Cyprus.
What a fucking idiot I was!

Two days after my dad passed away, my older siblings and I arrive back at my dad's house after the funeral.
If you are in an unfortunate position where you have to attend a funeral in a small village in Cyprus – don't go!
Smashing the coffin with rocks whilst it's going in the ground???? Come on people....what happened to "being laid to rest"?
As my older siblings and I approach my dad's house, we notice a hen is walking about the front yard. The house is set on a two acre plot and the hen-house is at the rear of the plot. I'm no poultry expert. It could have been a chicken.
I know my dad kept hens for eggs and chickens for barbeques and one thing neither of them do, is approach the house. Otherwise they too could be turning on a spit.
We pay no attention to tomorrow's Sunday roast and open the front door. The first to run into the house is the chicken/hen. The first place the chicken/hen goes to is my dad's armchair. She (I'm assuming it's a she because of the eggs) hops up onto the arm rest and just sits there. My siblings and I are gobsmacked! Of all the chairs the chicken could have sat on, she sits on my dad's.
It is a large open plan kitchen/dining room. My sister is on the three seater with my brother and I am on a stool by the breakfast island. There is another two seater and a random chair, but the chicken is on my dad's chair and we have just buried him.
We sit with open mouths looking in disbelief at a chicken.... sitting on my dad's chair.

It has no intention of moving.
My sister approaches it and starts to gently stroke the top of its head. It still sits there.
This was no messenger. It was my dad who came for one last visit.
A few hours later with the door left open due to the heat, the chicken (now with a red ribbon we tied to its neck so that no harm could ever come to it) jumps off the seat and scurries away.
My brother who remained in Cyprus whilst the rest of us went home to England said that the hen/chicken never approached the house again.

I apologise! This was supposed to be a quick mention, a brief account of my dad's funeral. I hadn't intended to stretch this out. I'll get back on track just after another quick story about something else that happened earlier on that day.

The funeral service was at our ancestral village church. The whole village turned out. Even one of my dad's lifelong enemies who (to his credit) arrived to say his goodbyes.
Now this guy attends this church week in week out for the past sixty years. On this particular day – the day of my dad's funeral service, this dude decides to fall arse over tit down the church's fourteen-odd concrete steps.
An old woman in black calmly turns to me and says, *<your dad pushed him!>*

Whilst I prepare for chapter 2 – feel free to go to Youtube and listen to Mike and the Mechanics -The Living Years. It's a song that now always comes to mind when I think about the old man.
There are some lines in the song that strike a chord. There's one line about not being there on the day my dad passed away and another which says how I did not say things I should have said whilst he was still with us.
I need to fix things so that I am not in this position again...buts it's hard.......

CHAPTER 2:-INTRODUCTION II

My name is Panico. In English you would (and some have to my annoyance) pronounced it as Pa-nii-co.
In Greek, or should I say, in Greek-Cypriot (I have visited many Greek Islands and nobody out there is called Panico. There are loads of Achilles and Adonis and Zorbas and Demis Roussos - but no Panico) you pronounce my name as Ban-ni-koh!
I don't know who started it. One day, somebody called me Pan and it stuck. I liked it, so I gave out my name as Pan.
<Hi, my name is Pan.>
I liked it until people thought Pan was too short, so they went and lengthened it with the following nicknames...
Frying-Pan, Chip-Pan, Bed-Pan, Dish-Pan, Pan-Cake, Peter-Pan, Shit-Pan, Pans-People (a 70s female dance group who would perform on Top-of-the-Pops whilst trying to avoid their fannies being touched-up by Jimmy Saville), Pan-doras Box, Pan-ic Stations, St Pan-cras Station, sPan-nahopitta (Greek for Spinach Quiche) Marzi-Pan, Psycho-Pan (explain that one later) and Banana-Head. Apparently, every time I would go outside to play in the street, I always had a banana in my hand!
After all these years, (man I am shaking even now) there is one nickname that still sends a chill down my spine. It nearly ruined my life. I could have killed the person who had said it initially – had I been eight to ten inches taller.

I took advice from a forum for self-publishers and will mention the name in Chapter 10- the primary school years so as to build some suspense and anticipation.

I was born in London in 1963, a borderline Cockney. Borderline because every time I asked my mum where I was born, she would say a hospital somewhere in East London. I asked what the name of the hospital was and her answer was always the same...she didn't know the name. I then asked her what she was doing in East London when she never ventured outside North London since her arrival to England. She couldn't answer. She happened to mention that, during that time, my dad worked in a Steak House in the East End of London.

To be a full Cockney you must be born within earshot of the sound of the Bow Bells. The Bow Bells are the Bells of St Mary-le-Bow Church in Cheapside East London.
On a quiet day, that sound would have travelled all the way to Highgate.
It was only later that I found out that dad had worked in East End Road which is in North London – hence why I say I'm a borderline Cockney!

It was often said, especially by my mum, that I was an ugly child with bandy legs. My mother would be pushing the pram down the street (North London) and when people would stop her to take a peep at the lovely baby, all they would see was a black mop of hair and Marty Feldman black goggle-eyes that were more fitting on a toad than on a baby.

Frog eyes was another nickname by the way!

I'd like to think that I grew into my looks and was less ugly to a point that I was able to get married to a stunningly beautiful woman who was not shallow to go for looks alone. However my look is what she did go for, because by the time I reached twenty-two, my goggle-eyes had sunk back into my eye sockets. That gave me this forever sad melancholic look, which made her feel sorry for me as one would a dopey eyed rescue dog.
She often says that she had rescued me from a depressing existence, where most evenings were spent spliffed up listening to my older brother listening to Pink Floyd.

I'm drifting in another chapter now, so let me pull back to introductions.

I've been happily married now for thirty years and have three great, well structured, very smart and very beautiful children. Depending on how long it takes to complete this book and self-publish on Amazon Kindle, I have two girls currently aged twenty-seven and twenty-five and a ten year gap between daughter number two and son number one (and only).
My son knows this part – I didn't really want a third child. I wasn't dead against the idea, but I had some concerns because we finally reached a good financial position after all those years of struggling with two kids in a tiny flat. We even started to have holidays.

Another concern I would tell the wife was that I didn't want a son as he would be ugly and teased like I was. Luckily for him, he has taken after my wife's family. At fifteen years of age, he is six-foot-one, with chiselled good looks and the body of an athlete. The nearest I came to athleticism was my athlete's feet.

Some people want to be rich or famous or have successful careers or all three. All I ever wanted was to be a good husband and a great dad. To be great parents....that's all.
This book's dedication says it all. I hope I have achieved or will achieve what I set out to be.

Right –enough of the soppy stuff!!!
Let's get on with the fun stuff..............

CHAPTER 3:-MAYTON STREET (OFF THE HOLLOWAY ROAD)

This is all from memory. I've had no collaboration which is why this early years chapter will be one of the shortest. It is not all bad as I've got this weird early set of memories – I even remember changing my own nappy - the old cloth ones with a few cotton balls chucked in the arse crack section.
If it is not a super memory, then it could have something to do with the fact that I stayed in Terry cloth nappies till the age of six. Either way, this is what I remember of this time.

The first place we had in Mayton Street was a rented first floor living area. Not to be confused with a flat. There must have been a kitchen and a separate toilet. Not sure about a bathroom though, but it doesn't matter, because nobody took baths in those days. If you needed a bath you either filled up the cast iron bucket and put it on the gas burner for three hours, or you'd take a trip to Hornsey Laundry and Baths – which is still there today, but it is a swimming pool.
I can't picture the kitchen or toilet (most likely because I never changed my own nappies in there), but I do remember the living-come-bed-room.
There was a small double bed for my parents, a foldaway bed for my older brother and sister to sleep head to toe in and the cot, which I had all to myself. There must have been a

television, but I can't picture it. The reason I know there must have been a television is because, on the wall by my cot was a Roger Moore picture calendar. It was screen shots of Roger Moore as The Saint (Simon Templar). In one picture, I remember the halo. So it makes sense that we must have had a television set- doesn't it?

It could be that my mum fancied the shit out of Roger Moore because he looked a bit like my dad with the quiff.

I always thought that my dad looked more like Christopher Lee. Anyway, whatever the reason for the calendar, it was good that the parents got on in those days. I think poverty does that to couples.

Warning sick joke coming up –

Due to Roger-Moore, more siblings were on the way so it was time to move to a bigger place.

Man that's weird – once again, I blame that on that Poloroid!

CHAPTER 4:-MAYTON STREET II THE GROUND FLOOR FLAT

It is never easy when you move to a new place. My mother was pregnant with kid number four so there was no choice but to uproot the whole family and move us two doors away to a ground floor flat – yes, a real flat with a garden.

It had a separate living room, a separate one bedroom with the same small double bed for my parents and a new single bed for my older sister. This time, my older brother and I had the fold down bed and the new baby boy was in my cot. Good luck with that kid - I crapped out the sides of my nappies so many times, that the goods were ingrained into the cot's soft wood.

No sooner had we settled into the new place and no sooner had my mother dropped baby number four, baby five was on the way. Go dad!!!

See poverty does that to couples. Maybe someone can explain to me why poor people tend to have more children? We have all seen the news footage of starving people in third world or war torn countries and we have all thought the same – why do they have so many kids?

I am not, nor would I dare to compare our situation to those in the worse possible conditions one can ever imagine. We had a roof over our heads and food (in the form bullybeef – tinned

meats with jelly) in our bellies and a mobile paraffin heater that twice nearly burnt the house down.
But in comparison to that kid who lived down our street with no dad but loads of generous uncles – yep we were poor.

So it wasn't long (nine months to be exact) before my little sister was born and she too joined us in our one bedroom that now slept seven.
During our time in this rented flat, we were seeing less and less of our father.
A couple of years after moving into this flat, my dad had opened up his own Greek restaurant in the Seven Sisters Road. He was working all hours and would come home early in the morning.
My mother for her part in his success would do all the laundry, not only for the five of us with the endless shitty nappies and the odd bed-wetted bedsheets, but also, all the restaurant tablecloths, chefs' jackets and tea towels. She would also cook some Greek Cypriot dishes like (no spell checker for these) Gobebggia, Koftethes and Sheftalies (that's stuffed vine leaves, meatballs and meat wrapped in lambs stomach membrane).

My mother would leave the older kids at home, grab me by the scruff, pack the young ones in prams and off we'd go with the dirty smelly laundry to Hornsey Baths, where three times a week, she spent a lovely evening washing, drying and then folding, with me at one end turning the sheets and table cloths the wrong way.

If I was lucky or proved to be totally useless at folding sheets, she would leave me at home with a slap and cart big sister off with her instead. And when big sister arrived home, she too would give me a slap.

If all the housework, cleaning, cooking and double laundry duties were not enough, my mother took in machinist work to bring in extra money to support the family and my father's restaurant business until the day when hopefully the restaurant took off.

A guy would drop off a large sack containing cut material. My mum, using a sample provided, would sew all the pieces together to produce various sizes of dresses or blouses. For the larger woman's size, she would end up sewing a tent!

To help out, we older kids were given knitting needles and our job was to turn the collars and belts outside-in. In other words, turn the seam inside so that it did not show. If you were heavy handed with the needle and you punctured the stitched item, you would get a slap.

It wasn't hard to grasp the connection – the more my mother worked and stressed – the more likely it was that one of us older kids would be in for a whack of some sort. In order to avoid a back-hander you either had to learn to (a) keep out of the way (b) don't make any mistakes in any chores you were given (c) you run.

Big brother chose (a), big sister took (b), but not always successful and I decided on (c)... I ran at every opportunity with some degree of success at first. I would head straight for the garden. The disadvantage of running away was that when you were caught, you would get twice the beating quota and if either or both siblings had pissed or stressed mum out, you would get their beats too.

The garden was a good sized plot with raised flower beds which allowed for strategic defensive battle maneuvers. My mother would use the offensive frontal assault and I would use the defensive trench warfare. Later she would learn and assimilate with her weapon of choice – the broom handle. She had the offensive close air support as the broom could swing at an arc over the raised beds and whack you on the arm. GAME OVER!

What strikes me as funny (apart from the broom handle hitting my humerus), was that somebody in the family took a photo of my mother chasing me around the garden. I don't know who took it, but I'm glad they found it amusing.
As you can see from the book's back cover (paperback edition), I've got the incriminating photo. I stole it from my mum's photo album for evidence, just in case somebody came up with the idea of a telephone number children could call twenty-four hours a day when they felt threatened with violence.
Sadly no such number existed then. Besides we never had a phone, so fat lot of good that number would have been.
If you study that photo, you would see me nervously standing on one side of the flower bed with my head facing my mother, but my feet turned the opposite way ready to scarper.
My mum is wearing her sewing machine overalls and has her running slippers on for jogging comfort. Her hands are in her pockets displaying the classic false illusion that she has no intention of chasing me. Then like a cheetah (Acinonyx

Jubatus), she would take off after her prey at sixty miles an hour.
During the spring and summer, the flower beds would act as a defensive barrier which I could run around in circles till one of us got dizzy. In the autumn and winter, when the beds had given up their harvest, mum would trample through them to get to me. In situations such as those, I would make for the garden wall. With knees scraping on bricks (I wore hand-me-down shorts for eleven months of the year), I would ungracefully leap into next door's garden for refuge.

Our next door neighbours were an Italian family. The Italian couple would pity me and on the many occasions when I landed in their garden – on my arse, they would offer asylum and protection. They even fed me spaghetti on one occasion.
They had two sons around my big brother's age and a daughter my age. It was the younger son that named me Banana-Head! My brother would go next door to hang-out with the Italian boys and when I would go round to join in, they would all pretend to be out. On a couple of occasions I played in the back garden with the daughter. That quickly ended when I tried to kiss her with snot running from my nose. She screamed and her brothers came out and chased me back over the wall into my garden and into my mother's waiting arms!

I remember the Italian lady one day looking over the wall asking my mum why she was chasing me. My mum recounted several reasons why I deserved a good smack – for being rude, or clumsily breaking a household item, or nicking money, making the little ones cry by taking their Farleys Rusks out of their little hands...

...yep, I was a little shit all right!

CHAPTER 5:-SATURDAY MORNING PICTURES

One Saturday big brother took me to Saturday Morning Pictures at the Holloway Odeon. It turned out to be two and a half hours of fun filled mayhem. You left one madhouse and entered another.
This was an introduction to a new world where, for a short period of time, you were free to not only escape any issues at home, but to run riot and let off a bit of steam....as well as to catch a cartoon in technicolour.
I was hooked.

Every Saturday morning there would be a long queue of impatient kids outside the entrance to the cinema, snaking and sprawling down the Holloway road. Gangs of kids would be pushing and elbowing each other, trying to get to the front and be first into the auditorium. It was imperative that you'd get there early and hold your ground by the main doors. Once the old usherettes opened the doors, a mad rush would ensue.
Kids ran inside like loonies with their hair on fire, in order to get seats at the back row or as near to the back as possible. Those who sat at the back were safe from projectiles such as chewing gum, sticky sweets or paper-made water-bombs. Those sat at the front rows were sitting ducks from the nutters sat behind.

Front-row-ers were often well-behaved newbies (Saturday Morning Pictures virgins) that would be accompanied by one or both parents, or god-forbid an old grandparent.
Middle-row-ers were smaller gangs of kids, unable to muscle into the back rows but well-adapt at throwing missiles.
The back row kids came with bigger brothers or larger gangs. The odd one would come with a girlfriend.

Once a kid experienced Saturday Morning Pictures, their Saturday mornings would never be the same again.
It was harmless chaotic fun, where kids could let off steam and meet with school friends. An old form of social-media-ing.
You would return to school on the Monday and discuss with your friends the movie you saw and who got hit and with what projectile. And come playtime, you would act out a scene from the feature movie.

Today, looking back, I am reminded of a scene in the film Gremlins. The scene where the Gremlins are crammed into the theatre fighting, jeering, swinging off lighting fixtures and throwing popcorn all over the place. They are interrupted by the sound of hammering and then the words "hi-ho" being sung by one of the dwarfs from Disney's Snow White and the Seven Dwarfs. The film begins to play on the big screen. Immediately, the Gremlins are silenced, then as one they all nod heads and start singing, "hi-ho, hi-ho, it's off to work we go." Then they all start swaying from side to side engrossed in the film and oblivious to the world around them.
That was Saturday Morning Pictures for me.

The Saturday morning program started with a cartoon, then a serialised 1940s cliffhanger like Flash Gordon starring Buster Crabbe.
Cliffhanger my arse though! At the end of an episode (or chapter as the movie-makers called it), it would clearly show Flash Gordon crashing his knob shaped spaceship into the side of Emperor Ming's arse-shaped palace and next week, we would be cheated by being shown the knob missing the palace and safely landing without a scratch on Flash's helmet.
The twelve chapter science fiction serial film was made in black and white and recorded in mono sound.
Flash Gordon (our hero) crash lands his rocket onto the planet Mongo. Throughout the serialization, Flash wears tight tops showing off his softening pectoral muscles.
His main squeeze, Dale Arden goes from a conservative 1940s outfit in chapter one, to a cleavage showing bikini top and Jodhpur bottoms from chapter two to twelve.
The bald Fu-ManChu looking villain was Emperor Ming the Merciless – ruler of planet Mongo.
Ming had a daughter called Princess Aura who had the hots for Flash (the hot flashes), but then stuck her claws into Prince Barin.
Prince Barin, who in a sci-fi film is dressed as Robin Hood, was a ruler of a region of Mongo called Arboria, therefore an enemy of Ming the Merciless.
Flash teams up with Prince Barin and Prince Vultan in an uprising against Ming.

Prince Vultan has wings! Well he needs wings as he is half hawk and his people (the Hawkmen) lived in a palace in the skies...
Oh-shit – nearly forgot Doctor Zarkov, the mad brilliant scientist who builds the knob-shaped space-ship along with a valve-powered radio transmitter. All through the chapters, Zarkov holds the radio transmitter's microphone calling out...
<Zarkov, calling Flash. Zarkov, calling Flash. Zarkov, calling Flash. Zarkov, calling Flash. Zarkov, calling Flash. Zarkov, calling Flash...>
Fucks sake, Flash is not answering. Your radio transmitter is the size of a house, where do you think Flash's radio receiver is?
Can you see where I am going with this?
Yep – they don't make em like they use ta!

Not related to "my" Saturday Morning Pictures, but staying slightly on topic – in 1974, some filmmaker made a Porno-spoof called Flesh Gordon. The rocket was indeed phallic shaped and the mission was to save the Earth from the deadly Sex-Ray bombarding the planet, which caused people to strip off their clothes and have sex till they died.
Doctor Zarkov was called Doctor Flexi Jerkoff (original) and the villain was Emperor Wang the Perverted.
Urban Legend warning: -
When I was young, big brother tells me that one Saturday morning, the projectionist showed Flesh Gordon instead of Flash Gordon to a cinema packed full of lucky kids.
In a time of no videos or internet to stream movies, this thought stuck with me for ages. When the time came when we

could afford a video player, one of the first films big brother and I rented out was Flesh Gordon.
<*Awkward cough.*> Anyway..er...back on topic.....

The next Saturday Morning Pictures feature, would be a short movie by the Children's Film Foundation (CFF).
What a treat it was to see clean middle class kids with a well-trained dog that didn't lick his own balls or pull the arms off the sockets of whoever was holding the dog lead at the time. The white middle class brats would ride bikes with baskets bolted to the handlebars, use compasses and carry rucksacks containing flasks of tea and Nana's homemade scones. They were home-schooled and had never set eyes on a Greek or black man.
The introduction to a Children's Film Foundation movie would silence the auditorium – if only for three minutes. The opening black and white scene was of a town square with a fountain and loud bells and birds scared into flight. It indicated that you were in for a dramatic treat.
Man I'm sounding bitter again...but remember, these are the thoughts of a young Pan. I need to get into my young head and write as young Pan would...hence the atrocious grammar.....(nice get-out old Pan)!
Ok it wasn't all about middle class posh kids solving mysteries. There was a few movies of scruffy poor orphans who would end up being adopted by a rich family after they thwarted the kidnapping of the rich family's pooch.
Anyway, nobody really paid attention to these movies past the opening scene. I always thought (not at that time though) that

these movies were government sponsored to inspire the working classes to better themselves and to instill acceptable behaviour, however once the opening scene ended and our ears stopped ringing, it was back to the masses throwing stink-bombs and popcorn, and running up and down the aisles trying to let off fire-extinguishers that were emptied months back.

The final slot was filled by the main feature film.
Some weeks they would show some right crappy movies. They may have been cheap for the cinema to buy in, but in the end it cost them double in cleaning and repair bills.
If it was a good action flick and there was a good battle or fight scene, feet would be stomped and back of chairs kicked in to exciting roars and cheers.
Any films that contained kissing would be met with a chorus of boos and hissing by the younger kids and shouts of *<get em off>* by the older kids.
At the end of the main feature, the curtains would close, the lights would slowly come on and the national anthem would play. We would all stand to attention, some with parade salutes and others with two finger salutes.

The best reaction to a movie which had us all sitting still and captured our imaginations was –The Seventh Voyage of Sinbad.
The worst ever reaction I witnessed to a film was Summer Holiday starring Cliff Richard.......say no more!

CHAPTER 6:-NIGHTMARES ON MAYTON STREET

The last years at Mayton Street proved to be the most challenging. We were seeing our father less and less and my mother was getting more stressed by the day. When I look back now, it amazes me how she coped.
Nope, coped is not right. It amazes me how she never ended up killing either herself, one of us kids or dad!
This is where I will make excuses for them both.

The hours my father spent at the restaurant were insane, but as he kept telling us whenever we happened to bump into him - he was doing this for all the family.
Sadly, what he was doing was tearing us apart and unknown then, driving us mildly insane.
Can you imagine, an immigrant with little knowledge of the language, with a harassed wife and five disheveled snotty kids, owning and running a (late night) restaurant in a tough part of North London in the 1970s.
Just to clarify snotty. I mean snot-covered not snooty like the kids in CFF films.
I remember my hand-me-down jumper sleeves being all stiff and covered with dried nasal mucus. They were handy though for blocking mum's blows with a broomstick-handle-come-rolling-pin. My greasy hair also had defensive properties. My mum's grip would often loosen and slip off during her one-handed grab as I would flee her clutches.

Lucky for me, I was not an only child and there were two older siblings who can share in the fun. Problem was, I had a grievance. To me at that time, it felt that the punishment was not being dished out equally. It wasn't fair. But then again, it could have been due to the fact that older brother was shooting up (getting taller, not taking heroin) and becoming a quiet kid. Older sis was doing double the house chores and tried to please as much as possible. She practically raised little sis with nappy changes and bucket baths...but sadly that would not help her in later years.

I was the rebellious one. I would say some cutting or stupid remark and with a hand twisted behind my back, mum would give me a slap on the head and dare me to say it again. So I would. And I would get another slap. And on it went. One of us was sure to yield and sometimes, that would be me. Not that I capitulated. It would be, when one of those slaps landed perfectly on my ear that would cause a pop sound. The perfect slap. A one-in-a-thousand. Impossibly hard to get right even if you wanted to. A fluke shot really.

For the ear pop effect, her palm would have to reach the optimum temperature and contain the right amount of sweat. My head needed to be at the correct angle which, and considering how I would be trying to pull myself out of the grip with head moving in all directions, only goes to prove how much of a fluke the ear-pop slap was (acronym'd to EPS).

The size of the ear is important as it would need to equal the palm area so that a perfect air-tight seal could be formed when the hand lands accurately over the ear.

Hand velocity is another factor.
Too slow and it won't cause compression, thus no ear pop (EP).
Too fast and the head momentum is such that you lose the seal causing less air pressure.
I am sure some smart-arse could come up with a scientific formula for EPS....
Talking about smart-arses... $EP = Ht/Hv \times \sqrt{(Ea2 \times Pa2)} \times \Pi$
Where Ht is hand temperature, Hv is hand velocity in centimetres per second and Ea/Pa is ear and palm area in centimetres!

It astounds me how she found the energy to chase me around the house when she had to contend with all that housework, the restaurant laundry, us, sewing garments to fit fat-arses and in particular, the late night (early morning) rows when dad would come home.

The one thing I am certain about is that it was not one day in particular that I can say - <*I remember being woken up by my parents' quarrelling,*> or, <*the first time I was awoken by shouts was after...*>
It was as if it had always been there, like walking. I don't remember the day I started walking. My parents do, but I don't. Hence, in this autobiography there is no chapter titled – The day I got up off my arse and walked.
My parents (my mum at least) must know the day, and likewise they may remember that there must have been a defining moment or an event or something burning inside them both which exploded out into a series of shouts, fights

and then beatings. Perhaps it was always there, since the first day they married – who knows.

It's hard to put this shit into words. I mean I'm not saying it is hard on me emotionally, just, it is hard trying to explain something which I am glad to say is alien to me. Alien to me that I could never in a million years understand why our parents would inflict their mess onto us. (*Our* –meaning my siblings and I, not you readers... However, I have begged some family members to pay the full kindle price.) Did they think we would walk away unscathed?
What I do know is that they must have had a mutual agreement dissolved. The agreement where they must not argue in front of the kids gone out the window! So rather than try and start this chapter with - *one night my parents started arguing late at night* - I could explain better the following way...

Have you ever gone to bed with a pit in your stomach knowing that tonight there was a chance you would be woken up...again?
I have.
I remember going to bed – all five of us kids at the same time, regardless of age due to our comfy sleeping arrangements.
Big sis had started to get changed under her own bed sheets. At least she had her own bed. The smaller siblings were tucked away in their cots and big brother and I, sharing a bed, had started kicking each other in the head – although I had the disadvantage when sleeping head-to-toe with a now taller lanky brother!

Many cold nights I would go to bed with socks on. Socks that I had worn continuously for weeks, so who was disadvantaged now brother?
Our mother was going to join us a few hours later once the television programme Hammer House of Horror finished.
She once let big brother stay up to watch Christopher Lee as Count Dracula and he in-turn described the whole film to me in gory detail. So if before there was a fifty-fifty chance of getting some kip, there was fuck-all chance of that now!
<D'you reckon they'll be at it tonight?> I would ask big brother - to no reply.

Have you ever woken up in the morning after a peaceful night's sleep, but were expecting a right shitty night?
Feels good doesn't it, or perhaps you know no different. I had that feeling hundreds of times in those days. Especially on weekends when you had no school. A lie-in and then tea and toast.
Talking about toast...you haven't lived if you have not eaten toast cooked on a paraffin heater. A paraffin heater for our posh readers is a portable combustible liquid filled heater that left black soot marks on the ceiling and made the house smell like a petrol station.
A van with a tank in the back filled with paraffin would drive around the neighbourhood and the guy driving would pull over and shout – *<OILLLLLL>* – and all us crazy kids would run out with two five gallon petrol cans and get them filled up by the guy with a fag in his mouth. Then we would run back indoors with the flammable fuel running down our hands and legs and

fill up the heater whilst it was burning away with that yellowish blue flame.
(Eureka moment) – *Shit, I just remembered the TV advert...it went Boom Boom Boom Boom, Essos Blue. The similarities to bomb-bomb-bomb says it all really. They were taking the piss!*
Anyway, I was talking about the best tasting toast ever.
First you would thickly slice a slice (reads weirdly) of bread. Not your square Hovis, but the round flying saucer shaped bread you could only buy from the Greek shop. It weighed five kilograms and stuck to your ribs so you wouldn't be hungry for a week!
You place the bread-brick on top of the steel mesh that covered the paraffin heater's burner and then you would just wait till smoke would rise off the bottom half of the bread. That meant it was ready to turn over. Once both sides were almost black, you run into the kitchen and dab some butter on it. There you have it – the best smelling and best tasting toast ever.
Just don't nick a fag out of your dad's packets (plural –he was a forty-a-day-man) and start smoking till at least an hour after refilling the paraffin heater - so that the fumes were totally dissipated.

Have you ever been woken up in the middle of the night by your parents shouting at each other and your younger siblings crying and all you could do is cower under the sheets and pray it won't last as long as the last time?
Yep, you guessed it...I have.
It was a battle with big brother as to who was able to pull the sheets over their heads, which was laughable really as we slept

head-to-toe (insert smiley face emoji). I would often lose that bedsheet tug-o-war and end up coiling up like a ball side-on to my brother's feet.

<Oh god they are getting louder.>

Nowadays, if you heard shouting or screaming coming from your neighbour's house, the police would arrive in no time. But this was the 1970s Holloway and a lot of us immigrant families were packed into these three story town-houses and were quite partial to a bit of wife beating now-and-again.

Sorry – just me sounding bitter again. Not all Greek Cypriots were wife beaters...only eighty percent of the ones I knew when growing up.

To be fair, I don't think my father was a wife beater. No excuses – but in those days things were different. Behaviours and outlooks were different. General consensus at the time was that the women stayed home and looked after the kids and the men went out to work, followed by a trip to the pub and then would come home and expect the meal to be ready on the table. In my dad's case, it was a visit to the Greek café where they served Greek coffee at the front of shop and played illegal poker at the back.

I'm digging a hole for myself – I know, I get it...

Anyway – you get my gist. I am in no position to educate you readers. You've seen my grammar and know too well that I'm not the sharpest tool. So to repeat...

To be fair, I don't think my father was a wife beater. But when I heard that first slap – I cried.

You would have thought that after that incident my mother would be off to the solicitors the next morning starting divorce proceedings. Hell, she might have done us all a favour (including my parents) if she had gone to a solicitor. But what if I was to tell you that a few days later I walked in on them at it.....

You never know, I might write about that in a following chapter, but I promise I won't make it too graphic as I may gag now as I did then.

Have you ever woken up in the morning after a shitty night listening to your parents fighting?

This is my fourth attempt at trying to explain marital conflicts and its effect on young children and like the previous three attempts, I am out of my depth. I can tell you that waking up in the mornings after a troublesome night was like waking up into a void. The room would be deathly silent. The young siblings afraid to make a sound and the older siblings too angry with their parents inflicting another miserable night on them. In silence, we would get dressed in the poky room and head out into the kitchen as stealthily as possible. In the kitchen we would not talk to each other and head out the door on our way to school with dark bags under our eyes.

Then we'd return from school as if nothing happened the previous night and things would seem normal until the next nocturnal misadventure.

Back then it was our family life. It did not feel normal so it was something you never spoke about to your friends or teachers.

As far as I knew, none of my friends went through the same thing. Who knows, maybe they all did. After all, is it that uncommon?
I should have gone into school that morning after a troubled night and said to my teacher <*Can I be excused from sums today Miss, as I had a right shitty night listening to dad shouting and mum crying?*>
Miss could have said - especially after I've just now googled the following academic paper on the effects of parents fighting on young children. The surmise is narrated as follows...
<*This is part of life Pan. Parents fighting could be deemed constructive as well as destructive. Did you know that kids who witness the worst of their parents' fights are prone to hostility and misbehaviour, not to mention nervousness and depression?*
However in some children Pan, some kinds of parental differences might actually help kids become better thinkers. If your parents fighting makes you feel less safe, it's bad Pan. But if your parents do not threaten your emotional safety, it might be a good thing.>
And I would say, <*oh right miss. So what you are saying is that in later years I could grow up to be a right bastard, a manic-depressive or I could grow up to be the next Friedrich Nietzsche... or closer to home, the next Aristotle?*>
<*Exactly Pan.*>
<*Well fuck me Miss. How about I merge the three for now and aim to be a sodding miserable smart-arse who goes around in a non-violent way vandalising the school and people's property in anticipation of which direction I eventually take in later life!*>

By Jove – I think I've cracked it at the fifth attempt!

I am ready to move on now.....to the next chapter...

CHAPTER 7:-TARZAN COMES TO MAYTON STREET

The guy who sold Tarzan to my father told him that Tarzan was a highly trained ex-police dog. Just what my dad needed to stand guard and protect the restaurant from break-ins and drunks. It didn't take long before my dad realised that this dog was suffering from some sort of post-traumatic-stress-disorder. Probably from seeing too much action during his crime fighting days. Of course nobody in the seventies was aware of such an illness as dog-PTSD.
My dad, on seeing the dog's head lolling from side to side after he had paid for it, swore in Greek. What my dad actually said was <*this faking basted dog is faking crazi*> (English translation is – <*I say old chaps, this dog is just not the full ticket.*>

The first week, Tarzan slept in the restaurant's back yard- the access for previous break-ins. Straight away this caused a problem as the kitchen staff couldn't go outside for a cigarette for fear of being pounced on by Tarzan. But that was the least of their issues. The kitchen staff could smoke behind the drinks bar if needed. The problem was the kitchen staff were not allowed to use the toilets used by the patrons as dad didn't want kitchen staff traipsing through the restaurant with greasy aprons and chef's hats on. Their toilets were outside!
Tarzan was outside and no amount of T-bone steak bones could bribe him into allowing the kitchen staff to have a shit unmolested.

Then there was the barking after the restaurant closed.
Tarzan never barked during the times the restaurant was open. The smell of the food coming out of the extractor fans seemed to relax Tarzan, knowing that every hour when one of the kitchen staff made a mad dash for the outside toilets, he would get a bone. These T-bones had meat on them as customers were just too posh to handle the steak with their hands to pick the meat off.
But when the extractor fans fell silent and the restaurant closed, this stressed out Tarzan and he would bark from four in the morning till the evening when the smell of cooking resumed.
The people living in flats above the shops in the area complained to my dad. Unable to control or keep Tarzan at the restaurant, dad decided to bring him home as a pet for us kids.

The guy who convinced my mum to take the dog in told her that Tarzan was an ex-police dog, who retired from the force and lived with a family on a farm and that the family were relocating to Australia and couldn't take a dog with them. Tarzan would make a great pet, keep us kids occupied and protect the family from any Turks.
The lady who told us kids that morning that dad was bringing us a pet after school was the best lady ever!

We were going to get a dog just like the one in those CFF films they played at Saturday Morning Pictures.
I was going to teach him to fetch, lift his paw and lick his balls on command. I was making plans to add to the obstacle course

in the garden - the course that served me so well during war games with mum.
I had this image in my head of me on one knee in a field and an arm around Tarzan's neck. I made plans (on paper) to go camping – just me and Tarzan, pitching a tent in Finsbury Park.
Like the canine movie star Lassie, Tarzan would bark on any approaching winos and snarl at bullies. And if I got my foot caught in a bear-trap or if I fell down a disused goldmine shaft, Tarzan would run off and fetch help!
I'd be Tarzan's favourite and he would wait outside the school gates all day and when school finished, we would walk home together.

My older siblings and I were by the front window eagerly anticipating Tarzan's arrival. My dad was to bring him home any minute....now............................and then we heard something...........barking......and shouting....shouting in Greek. There was a commotion further up the road just out of visual range. I saw children running..........I saw a wolf's head..........a snarling wolf with a thick chrome chain around its neck. Attached to the chain was a long leather lead and it was dragging somebody behind.
Is that my dad?
I've never seen him so disheveled. He always wore a suit, shirt and tie. Now the shirt was half way up his back and the jacket half way down his arse. He seemed to be on ice skates. He was slipping and sliding and stumbling along the footpath, being

dragged at speeds which I never dreamed my dad could achieve.
I heard him swear in Greek <*TARZAN FAKS SAKEEE.*> (translation) <*Tarzan for crying out loud.*>
We saw curtains move behind windows.
I imagine the neighbours were saying something like <*it's those bloody immigrants again.*>
Tarzan sprinted straight past our house and dad let one hand go off the lead and made a grab for our front garden gate.
I heard shoulders pop.
No, it was just next door's door knocker being rattled by our neighbour, desperate for somebody to let him in before Tarzan reached his house and ripped him a new arse-hole.
My dad held tight and managed to slow the dog down and then started to reel him in towards our front garden.
My younger siblings hearing the noise started crying.
My mum came up to the window and screamed out <*ton thkiaolo ton mavro.*> (translation- *the devil is black).*
The devil featured a lot when my mother swore.
<*Kleíste tes pórtes,*> she shouted. My siblings and I looked at each other scared and confused. Then we understood. She meant close all the doors leading off the hallway – including the room we were in.
The ground floor flat had a hallway leading from the front door to the back garden door with the kitchen, living room and our one-bedroom-that-slept-seven leading off it. My mum made a dash for the kitchen door and closed herself in. The older siblings made a dash for the living room and I was shit-scared

to budge, but managed to close the bedroom door and make a dash back to the window.
The younger siblings' cries intensified after seeing their mum flee for the kitchen.
I bet she had that broom in her hand. If she did...god help Tarzan. She managed to get me on the funny bone a few days back and my elbow was still tingling!

Dad had managed to seize some sort of control and diverted Tarzan up our garden path. I saw Tarzan lift up on his hind legs and then..........
The rest of this tale is now based on audio deduction as I lost visual on first Tarzan and then my dad.

I heard Tarzan's two front paws slam on the front door, followed by scratching up and down it. I heard the key go into the Yale lock after several attempts and then the front door crashed against the hallway wall. I heard the three glass pendant ceiling lights clinking against each other due to vibrations pulsating through the house. The bedroom door shuddered. I heard my dad slipping, losing grip on the worn linoleum flooring. There was a sticky tearing sound, most likely the tape joining the sections of lino together as the landlord was such a tight arse; he couldn't spend the money on one single piece but many off cuts taped together with black electrical insulation tape.
The sounds were now coming from further down the hallway.
I was almost safe.

More ripping and scratching sounds. The patterned wallpaper was being torn. I doubt if anybody could tell the difference anyway. And then a scream............ <THKIAOLOOOOO!>
It was my mother screaming <*DEVILLLLLL...!!*>
My father had managed to get Tarzan to the back door. This next bit was going to be tricky as the hallway narrowed down at the rear of the house and Tarzan had reached the back door first. There was no room for my dad to squeeze past.
Like I said, I had no sight of what was going on however I think my dad straddled Tarzan like John Wayne getting on a horse. (The later John Wayne films where he was just about able to mount one).
CRASH! That was the back garden door window followed by the dodgy window putty falling. The putty had yet to dry after the last time the window was replaced when mum put the broom handle through it!
The dog was out in the garden.

< *HE DID IT,*> I shouted <*THE SON OF A BITCH DID IT!*>

(All right, all right, I didn't really shout that out. I googled famous triumphant quotes and got this one from the sci-fi movie Independence Day... the scene where Randy Quaid pilots his jet at the heart of the alien space ship's weapon causing the alien craft to explode and us humans win the war.........).

Sadly Tarzan's stay with us was not to last the month out. The neighbours all signed a petition and the landlord threatened to evict us. The garden was out of bounds and I had trouble finding an escape route when chased for a beating. The choice was the broom handle or running through the minefield of Tarzan's shit and/or having one of my arse-cheeks chewed. It was a close call, but I opted for the broom.

What happened to Tarzan I hear you dog lovers ask?
Well apparently, that lovely family that lived on the farm who were going to move to Australia ended up staying and took Tarzan back..........or so my mum says!!

CHAPTER 8:-BATHTIMES

To say we stunk back then is an understatement. Me in particular! A simple way to know if my clothes needed washing was to chuck them against the wall...if they stuck, it was time for a change. To see if my underpants required a soak in bleach, again, I would chuck them against the wall and if my pants ran away, then they were way past due for a peeling.

It wasn't that I relished smelling like a shit-house or that I preferred eau-de-paraffin to eau-de-cologne....or in my case, eau-de-toilet (eau-de-bog) to the smell of Rothmans King Size. The reason I stunk is that I hated and loathed bathtimes. I was shit-scared of bathtimes. Yeah I would get beats during bathtimes, but I was used to beats...I became immune to them. It was being semi-naked and getting slaps that I couldn't accept.

There is something about being hit when you are (semi) naked. Somehow you feel defenseless compared to having clothes on. Explains why Japanese POWs were stripped naked during torture and that's how I felt during the times I stood in the bathtub.

The most annoying thing was that it was not my behaviour (this time) that drove my mother to punish me, but the fucked up water heater, which by all accounts should have killed us all long ago by carbon-monoxide poisoning.

Venting gas appliances by means of a flue had yet to be invented back then!

After many complaints and a few threats from my dad, the landlord complied and finally got the old Ascot water heater repaired in the bathroom.
Yippee, no more boiling water in cast iron buckets.....well fuck you Mister Landlord!!!

I was around six or seven years old and I was able to sponge-wash myself using the hot water from the bucket standing in the bath. However, using the Ascot proved to be a right bastard. It was mounted high on the wall above the bathtub and had a rubber hose attached to the spout which they run into the tub. Hey we invented the mono-shower.
But I couldn't reach the Ascot and I cursed (in Greek) the Pesevengi, Malaka who installed it.
Sorry, I hardly swear in Greek unless it is aimed at a Greek.

I know a lot has been written about what the Greeks have given humanity (medicine, mathematics, giving but not taking one up the arse), but what you non-Greek speakers are perhaps not aware of is that we Greek Cypriots mastered the art of swearing. We have a swear word for every occasion including masculine and feminine swear words.
Malaka is our most popular and classics of all the masculine swear words. Malaka is a mainland Greek word for wanker, but no ordinary wanker- a dumb-arse wanker, who probably wanked himself stupid.
Now Pesevengi (excuse the spelling) is a Cypriot favourite used by Greek and Turkish Cypriots alike.

It means pimp, but no ordinary pimp. A Pesevengi would only pimp out his mother or sister...or both and would not charge much for the pleasure.
If I get time and space at the end of the book, I may educate you with some more Greek and Greek Cypriot swear words that you can use when you go to Agia Napa.

That bloody Ascot- not only couldn't I reach the damn thing, but it was temperamental and erratic because of its actions, and which all O'level students know, actions have equal and opposite reactions (Newton's Third Law I think). In other words, when the Ascot fucks-up, I too get fucked up.

I couldn't operate the water heater and my mum refused to heat anymore water in buckets, so I had to be bathed...by her. I point blank refused to be bathed. I was going to stick to that decision no matter how many slaps I got. However, in the end I lost out to Newton's Second Law –the acceleration and force of a slap in contrast to my skinny arse sent me flying.
Cannot think of how to include Newton's first law...so I won't bother. Shame really, would have been a nice ending to this chapter...
In the end, I agreed to being bathed providing I kept my Y-fronts on.

I would hold the rubber hose up high and water would gush out over my head and shoulders and run down my back. The bathplug was missing (I think I used it once in the old Butler sink out in the garden, where I kept my tadpoles and misplaced

it) so I had to keep one foot on a flannel over the plug hole. That way, I could sit in the tub (with my pants on) and get my arse soaked too.
My mum would be standing there adjusting the f-ing Ascot's thermostat in coordination with my shrieks.
Before you say it, we did try and fill the bath up with water using all kind of objects to block the plughole but none worked and by the time I was ready to jump in, almost all the water would have gone.
Mono-shower (to repeat –which we invented) was the only option.
Oh knock it off – I know what you're thinking....why not buy another plug for the hole? This is the 1969/70s...there is no flipping B&Q or Homebase or Screwfix... so let me get on with the story...
<Mum – too hot,> I'd shout, so she would turn the thermostatic dial one way...
<NO – too cold now.> Then the dial turned the opposite direction.
<TOO HOT.> Slap!
Like I said, there is something totally dispiriting and crushing about being hit on a naked back.
<TOO HOTTTTT.> Puff of air from her lips, then slap followed by a curse aimed at the Ascot.
<That's it, leave it, leave it, it's good. Go away now.>

Mum would walk away to the kitchen which gave me some private time to get that sponge way down my arse crack and up and down my balls with one hand whilst the other was holding the hose.

Yeah, I had balls! Small ones, which would seek refuge within my under-carriage, but they were there.

The water was warm and I was starting to feel the benefits of bathing as the water running off me was a different shade of brown. I gave my neck (although I couldn't see it but was told many times that it was black) and my ankles an extra scrub.

As my body soaked in a warm downpour from the hose I held, I would start to pull my pants away and examine (like all boys do) my willy. I would pull at the skin folds at the top and look for the hole where the wee came from....

Just then, the door opened and I heard my sister's scream.

I screamed too and then when I looked up and saw my sister storming out the bathroom, I would scream again.

<*Get outttttttt!*> I screamed again...even though she was no longer in the bathroom.

<*Thkiaolo ton.*> From the kitchen, my mother would scream at the devil again...or was it at me?

<*I want to go to the toilet,*> my big sister screams from the hallway, <*tell him to hurry up.*>

<*I haven't finished yet...stupid cow.*>

<*Yes you had - you were playing with your billou!*>

<*I WASN'T PLAYING WITH MY BILLOUUUUUUU.*>

<Hahaha, was Panico playing with his willy?> My big brother would join in.

<I WASN'T PLAYING WITH MY WILLYYYYYYYY.> I would protest.

<*Billou-player.*> Big sister shouts.

<Billou-player.> Big brother shouts and laughs.
<*SHUT UP*,> and then in Greek I call out <*Milkman's daughter*!>

As I angrily gestured, I would lose control of the hose and water would go all over the floor.
<*Mum. Panico called me Milkman's daughter again.*>
<*What did you call her*?> Mum shouts angrily in Greek from the kitchen.
<*Nothing...*> which came out as a whimper.
<*I heard him mum,*> big brother pipes up. <*He called her that again.*>
<*No I neverrrrrrrr..........*>
Shit, the water's getting cold...too cold – <*Muuuummmm!*>
<*One minute, I'm changing your brother's nappy.*>
<But the water's cold.....>

My mum rushes in holding my little brother naked from the waist down. She sees the water all over the floor. She feels the water coming from the hose and then gives me an open hand slap on my back. She moves the Ascot's dial and leaves the bathroom holding little brother with shit up his back.
<*MUUUUMMMM TOO HOT NOW!*>
This time I would stand up with soggy pants slowly sliding back down. Stretching to reach up high, I would bang at the side of the Ascot heater with one hand while water poured out the hose I'm holding with the other hand.
The water starts to cool, then turns cold and then, ice cold.
I'm stood their shivering as cold water runs down my legs.

It’s so cold, I lose control of the hose and send more water out the tub once more. This time, my balls have taken refuge with my kidneys!

My mother enters the bathroom holding a wooden spoon. Water goes all over her feet. Little brother is screaming from the kitchen and big sister shouts out that little brother has rolled off the table onto the floor and a nappy pin has stuck into him.
Mum turns the taps off and raises the wooden spoon.
I clamber out of the tub and slip on the water and land on my hand and knees. Mum waves the spoon and takes aim, but I’m too low down for her to land a decent shot.
Keeping low, I crawl out of the bathroom sogging-wet, trailing sagging soggy underpants behind me. There is a slug-trail leaving the bathroom into the hallway.
I look up and see big sis in the hallway laughing at me so I mouth the syllables in Greek <*Milk-man’s-daugh-ter.*>
Actually, there’re far more syllables said in the Greek translation.

<*Come back here.*> Mum would shout...
<*Fuck no – and fuck that Ascot!*>

CHAPTER 9:-PAKEMAN STREET I

Hard work pays off in the end. The sacrifices you make, the time spent away from the children, the rows, the stress, the dysfunctional family you've unprepared for the real world, the future counselling, the neglect, the tears and the nightmares, all could be the price you pay for success.
There is no doubt that both parents - immigrants who arrived in England with two small children, no money and a worthless dowry - achieved something remarkable.
It was time to leave the one bedroom flat that sleeps seven and move to a three story townhouse. A townhouse paid (mortgaged initially) by the sweat of both parents.
The restaurant was doing well, my father was turning in a profit and was becoming a successful and important man in the community. The time came where he could not be seen renting a small one bed flat off the local greengrocer.
The house will show them all that he finally has arrived.
More on the restaurant(s) later...

I don't remember packing or moving the distance of one hundred and seventy metres from Mayton Street to Pakeman Street. I don't remember any build-up of excitement or any prior discussions. I do remember materialising with my big brother in a hallway of a house and being told that our room is the attic.

<*An attic –what's that?*>
My brother led and up we went, one landing after another, after another, then through what looked like a cupboard door, then up a narrow steep twisting staircase to the attic, our bedroom with two single beds. *One each*!!
The ceilings sloped on both sides, and there was a window. We both rushed to it and looked out. We saw gardens, and garden walls and trees and roofs and a church spire. There were tower blocks in the distance, we saw the Hornsey road and we saw the clouds - almost in touching distance.
Up here in our new bedroom, we were nearer to the heavens and it felt great.
I remember going up into the attic was easier than coming down. As you walked up the winding stairs, the top step was level with the attic floor level, almost in the middle of the room. This meant as you approached the stairs to go down, you could look over the edge of the floor space and see the drop to the bottom step. That shit me right up. For the first six months, I would have to shuffle on my backside along the attic floor towards the top step and go down each step on my arse, till eventually my feet would hit the third floor landing. A minor inconvenience really considering the tiny place we left behind.

This new house was massive. Three floors, not including the attic. Every wall was covered in wood-chip and every inch of it painted magnolia. There were doors everywhere, all new and clean and boarded with a white material that the builder told my father was fire-proof and would protect the whole family

in an event of a fire. There was new lino on all floors and no tape sticking halves together.
As I look back now, I can remember how that house looked in pristine condition. Sadly that is the only time that house would look that way. In later years, my younger brother would see to it that every door panel was kicked in, every plaster wall punched-in with little fist sized holes that would grow into man-size holes, and not only fist sized but head-sized too. Obviously, this would not happen overnight but a gradual increase over a period of time. A period of increasing anxiety and a cry of help from a child that we all let down.

If you are reading this....I'm sorry. I tried to be there for you... honest. But I was young...and stupid. What did I know of these issues? And in the end, I bailed out, I had to, otherwise I'd still be there....with you.

On the second floor, my father had the builder turn the smaller of the bedrooms into a kitchen and the larger room into a living room/come bedroom. His plan was to rent the second floor out so that the tenants would help out with the initial mortgage payments. Well that was the idea....didn't work out that well in the end.
The first floor double room at the front was to be the girls' bedroom and little brother would have the adjacent smaller room. The toilet was between the ground and first floor level. On the ground floor, the front room became my parents room...till they kicked the tenants out and it was all change again.

There was a further living/dining room and a kitchen. Also the family bathroom and toilet was on the ground floor.

As luck would have it, the sleeping arrangements lasted about a year or so and when the tenants left, I ended up having the attic all to myself.
I don't know who that couple were, except they were Greek Cypriot. The guy worked for my dad and he too would slap his wife in the middle of the night..........what luck!!!

Have you ever gone to bed in your new house and expected to get a peaceful night's sleep, only for it to be disturbed by a fighting married couple who were not your parents?
There was something different about this couple's fighting. There wasn't that atmosphere, the darkness, the accumulation of fear or that dread that you felt when my parents went at it. Obviously, I didn't feel that because these two clowns were not my parents, but clowns they were, in fact, there was something comical about these two "having a barney" (Barney Rubble- trouble).
It was later when we were reminiscing with my big brother after my dad's funeral...you know, talking about the old days in the attic, when we both realised that the lady in question like to be slapped around during sex.
Don't look at me like that, I'm not making a joke out of domestic violence. It is after you go over the events when you are much older that you realise that your young mind did not comprehend the true nature of adults' actions. For example, I told my mum that dad was being rude to our friend and

neighbour who frequently popped round for coffee and a gossip. All three never spoke to each other for months.
Later you come to understand that poking ones tongue out to a lady can have other connotations.

So my brother and I are sleeping in our bedroom, when we are both awoken by arguing below.
We hear the Greek word *<Pushti-iiiiiiii,>* then followed by a slap. (Pushti is a derogatory word for homosexual, but can also be used amongst friends, or in this case to demasculinise someone with a small dick!
There would be sobs, but not the cries we would hear our mother make. These were childish, girlish cries. They didn't feel like the real thing – we should know.
<Pushti, Pushti.>
Now why would she go and call him that again? He's only going to....Slap!!
And then a rhythm would commence, a tempo of cries of *<Pushti>*, a slap, a sob and moans.
This shit would increase in volume and speed and then inappropriately reach a climax!
Not sure which I preferred - the parents or these two idiots. The only saving grace was that in our new house, I didn't have my brother's cheesy feet in my face!

A year later, that couple moved out and everyone moved up one floor, except my big brother, he moved down one. My parents had the double room at the front of the first floor, the girls on

the second floor front and big brother second floor rear. Little brother as he was.
Having your own room was great, but lonely and non-comforting, especially as now that the parents moved up, we stopped listening to the clowns at it, and went back to the real thing. How the professionals do it – domestic violence at its best. Into the early hours, frighteningly and more harrowing in a bigger house with high ceilings. It gave those shouts and screams that reverberation – like music in a church, except there was nothing heavenly about it. And when you hear that belt crack like a whip for the first time, you know that even God must have looked away.

Hard work does pay, but with hard work, comes time spent away from the family which harbours suspicion and doubt and resentment. You would have thought financial success would heal certain wounds and relieve some pressure, alas, this is not shown (with my parents) to be true. Financial security plugged a small hole in the many holes that were leaking water from this dam they called a marriage. When the dam eventually burst, there was just too much damage done to save anything worth saving.

We never, ever went out as a family. We had no family holidays and no family trips to the zoo. We never missed out or felt different because we knew no different. In the end, I think we kids (especially the older ones) became accustomed to our parents late night/early morning conflicts.

The following day, you'd bump into your parents and they'd behave as if nothing had happened, so you thought, *yep – good morning parents – what do you have planned today? Another normal average day*?

CHAPTER 10:-PRIMARY SCHOOL YEARS - SHORT STORIES...

For timeline continuity, I need to pause the Pakeman Street chapter and insert a bit on primary school. I can't finish the Pakeman Street chapter and go back to primary school because I need to get into a mindset...find the child in me whilst writing along a timeline of sorts.
Now that I'm thinking about it, I'll probably have further breaks during Pakeman Street for secondary school and others. We will see as I go on.

Not sure if you can see from the book cover, but along with being a bit smelly - but not the smelliest... (Man we had some bed-wetters at school) I was a scruffy one, that's for sure.
I wore hand me down clothes with sticky sleeves.
Along with bathtimes, I hated haircuts too, so during my primary school years, I went from a smelly clean-cut kid (one of the old senile neighbours said my haircut used to resemble Clark Gable's) to having a greasy mop almost down to my shoulders. The only haircut I had during primary school was after I decided to cut my own hair so I could look like The Slade's guitarist's Dave Hill. I thought I looked cool, but everyone (parents, siblings, teachers, the milkman, the guy who came round to collect the Football Pools money, everyone

at Saturday Morning Pictures, the corner shop owner, the lady who said I use to look like Clark Gable) started to take the right piss, that eventually I capitulated and went with my dad to his barbers.
Dad had a Roger Moore cut and a splash of Pashana on the back of his clipped neck and whilst I asked for a Brian Connelly look (lead singer of The Sweet), I ended up with a Cypriot National Guard buzz-cut. I went ape-shit or in other words I started crying. The barber ignored my protests and pointed over to two orphan looking fat kids with the same death row haircut and said <*Now you look smart like my sons.*>
<*Well one day, your sons and I will have it out,*> and funny enough a few years later we did!

* * *

Miss Boo

What baffles me after describing the above is how I became teacher's pet........... (*The dots mean I am going into thinking mode.........*)
One day, that very same teacher did something that nearly wrecked my whole life.

I liked Miss Boo. Looking back now, I am almost certain her name was not Boo. It was probably Boon or Beau, but I remember calling her Boo.
She was pretty and dressed in bright purple clothes and she smelt nice. Unlike other teachers, she never shouted or hit us

with the ruler. It's not a cliché, we really did get hit with rulers in primary school.

I went from being mischievous and disobedient to skipping around like an idiot every time Miss Boo called my name.

My name went from Panico to Pani to My Pani, but I didn't mind. I had all those nicknames, what was one more. Besides Pani sounded much better than Frying Pan I was getting at the time.

It was during school play rehearsal when Miss Boo did what she did and nearly ruined my whole life and not just school - year two. It was during the dress rehearsal, when I was taking my jumper off to get into my moon costume. I was playing the moon and I had an important line – pivotal to the whole play.

<Hello, I'm the moon,> was my line.

Don't take the mick! Others never had lines, they just sung in groups or wore sun-masks and pranced about. I had a line!

We were in the school hall. The whole class was there, but all the other kids were running around mucking about. Not me though- I took my part seriously.

Miss Boo took me to one side. She was holding my costume and looking at me in a way no lady ever had. I mean she never had that – I'm gonna slap you look –

<Take your jumper off Pani so I can slip this on,> she said.

So I pulled at the sticky sleeves first and once my arms were free, I pulled the rest of the jumper over my head. I looked down at my string vest I was wearing underneath and noticed a great big hole in the middle of my chest. I went red with embarrassment.

Miss Boo giggled whilst raising her finger to her mouth.........
.... <*What are we to do with you Pani-Blossom,*> she whispered.
Actually she didn't whisper...
<*PANI-BLOSSOM!*> one of my classmates shouted as he happened to be running past that very second.
<*PANIBLOSSOMMMM!!*> He shouts again whilst pointing a bogie-tipped finger at me and laughing.
The whole class stopped and gawked. It went quiet and then they caught onto the new nickname and in unison they all pointed and laughed and called out <*PANIBLOSSOMMMM!*>

A few years back, I was sat at the dining table with my wife and kids and I was telling this story. I thought they would laugh, which they did, but what I never expected was for my son, forty seven years later, to start calling me Pani-blossom.

* * *

Headlock

That year was a nightmare. It would end a nightmare and following years would continue to be so........or so it would have had I not had a fight...and won! I then realised that I was good at fighting (until I reached secondary school, and man did I get the shit beaten out of me) and fighting resolved a lot of issues at primary school.
Being called Pani-blossom stopped that's for sure.
During one fight, I ended up getting a kid in a headlock, the same way the wrestler Mick McMannus would get his opponents into. I then discovered, nobody could get out of my

headlocks, therefore armed with the weapon of choice, I proceeded to have many successful fights with kids my age thereafter.
The one fight I did lose was due to having a fractured arm which made headlocking impossible. I broke my arm by performing a Judo side break-fall on concrete.

I don't know whether it was the times we lived in or perhaps the neighbourhood I grew up in, or poverty or both, but there sure were a lot of school fights, especially for a primary school. As fighting was an integral part of school life, I begged my parents to allow me to join the same Judo classes my best friend at the time use to attend.
I loved Judo. I thought I was good at it. My parents said they couldn't afford to buy me my own Judogi (a Judo uniform), so I would have to hire one out from the club – two sizes bigger. I would take the bus on my own to Highbury Corner and walk the five minutes to the club based at Highbury School.
I learnt how to break-fall (which actually works as stated earlier). I learnt how to perform Judo throws like the Deashi Harai (a leg sweep), the Tai Otoshi (body throw) and a Tsuri Goshi (hip throw). My favourite moves were the floor grapple holds, where I could put my headlocks on and hold on for dear life, even after the Sensei would shout at me to let go!
I reached a yellow belt and then I stopped when Sensei told me off for wiping my snot on the hired-out Judogi.
I wasn't good with authority or blowing my nose!

You may have noticed that this chapter's subtitle (Headlock) story isn't going anywhere. Those astute of you would have noticed that, I am keeping something back and you'd be correct. It is something that happened that I have never told anybody since leaving primary school....something that I am totally ashamed to talk about.
Yes I am worried what you guys would think of me, even if I said it was the times I lived in, or it was an accident and I got caught up in the moment...or, if I said that this girl was no girl but a harden bruiser who terrorised every schoolkid in the playground.....you wouldn't believe me. You would try and psychoanalyse and say that this action is a correlation to what I witnessed at home ....but you'd be wrong. It just happened... and for what I am about to write, I humbly apologise especially to my wife and kids..... But I was only eight........!!

She was no ordinary ten year old girl. She was tall and wide with tight curly ginger curls (cliché warning) and always wore denim dungarees. A lot of kids said that she had a knuckle-duster in the front dungaree pocket, but that could have been bullshit – to scare us off.
On either side of the middle patch pocket were round builder's boobs.
She was the best girl fighter in all the school and the best fighter of boys aged up to eleven. She once picked up this skinny year three boy and reverse bear-hugged him with both hands clasped behind his scrawny torso; she squeezed him so tight, that two snot-bubbles blew out from each of his nostrils, with one of the bubbles making a pop sound when it burst, whilst the other snot-bubble just deflated slowly.

Another time, she went behind a year two boy and pulled down his shorts and his pants in one swift pulldown action. As if that wasn't embarrassing enough for that kid, she then proceeded to point out to everyone the kids brown skid-marks running from the rear label to the front of the Y in his Y-fronts. That kid was not seen for a whole month after that.

One day she set her sights on me.
I was strutting around in a new Adidas T-shirt my mum had got me from Holloway Market. For once, not a hand-me-down. She walks up to me (followed by the rest of her gang) and starts digging at each letter on my t-shirt with her powerful pointy finger and shouts <*A.D.I.D.A.S- A Dog Is Doing A Shit*> and for those thickkos who never got it the first time (me included) she repeats it, only this time louder... -
<*A.D.I.D.A.S- A Dog Is Doing A Shit...are you doing a shit, dog?*>
I came back at her with the best retort I could think of...
<*Shut up fatso,*> I said.
She lunged at me with both arms spread open. I ducked, side-stepped and reached over her neck with my left arm and managed to arc it around her thick neck, where I quickly grabbed my left wrist with my right hand and bent her down. The headlock was engaged. Her head was under my arm, twisted to one side looking up at me.
Statistics showed that I won 100% of all scraps if I managed to lock in the headlock within the first two minutes of a fight. I had achieved it in under one. The fight was over.....or so I thought.

I don't know if it was her thick neck, or that my fractured arm had not healed properly, but I was losing my grip. She started to straighten her back and the lock was slipping.
I Pan-icked!
Please don't judge me...........
I was going to lose the fight the moment she became free.
My right hand slipped off my left wrist and as it became free, I swung my right hand back and threw a soft-ish right hook.
-Oh god it connected so well....with her nose.......
The girl cried out. Her gang cried out. The teachers, who upon seeing the circle of kids in the middle of the playground, made their way to the centre at the exact moment my punch connected to gush of blood.... well they cried out too.

It comes as no surprise that when the time came to choose a secondary school, there would be no choices. It would be an all-boys school.........for my sins!

* * *

Special shampoo

One day we all had to line up outside the nurse's office.
One by one we were called in and eventually it was my turn.
I walked in and was asked by a tall thin lady to stand by a trolley and look straight ahead. There was a strong smell of Dettol and piss and I was just about to make a comment, when another well boned lady takes a comb out of a glass of liquid

and starts combing my hair. She struggled at first, but eventually succeeded in completing a downward motion from hair-parting to shoulders. She tilts my head one way and then the other and then puts the comb down and with gloved fingers rummages through my mop like Tarzan's monkey Cheetah (that's Johnny Weissmuller's Tarzan, not the ex-police/special forces dog called Tarzan).
The lady combing my hair tuts, then harrumphs and motions to the first lady to come and look at my head. I can see the thin lady shaking her head then she bends down, picks up a cardboard rectangular package containing a bottle from the trolley's bottom shelf, puts it in a brown paper bag along with an envelope and hands it to me.
<Give this to your mother.>
<What is it?>
<Special Shampoo for being a special boy!>

I've never been called *special* before. I make my way to my classroom feeling somewhat content with life. I remember thinking that I would have preferred a tube of Smarties, but hey, who am I to refuse any kind of award.
I strut into the classroom with a shit-eating grin on my face holding out my prize, making sure the whole class can see that I returned with a gift. When I noticed that no other kid had a brown paper bag, my grin widened and my chest puffed out. One boy tried to grab the bag, but I pulled it back towards me with lightening reflexes and barked *<MINE!>*

Hindsight's a wonderful thing and so is reading the label before one starts to brag to the whole classroom. With so many knocks during those early school years, I deserved a bit of a change in circumstances, a short period where I was not the brunt of misfortune. A bit of time where I held onto a secret and courted some positive attention for once. A time when the rest of the class finally considered me as an equal and not some dumbass-fuckwitt.

I will keep them guessing about my prize all day. Who knows maybe they will think that I was special, maybe they will..................<*Oi, where's my reward?*>

No sooner had I placed my special gift on the table to pull my chair in, my then best friend grabs the bag, pulls out the cardboard box and then pulls out the bottle, all this before I even had the chance to push my chair back out. The little shit then reads out loudly the writing on the bottle's label....

<*Treatment - for head lice and nits!*>

I was confused. My then best friend was confused, actually the whole class was confu..............

<*FLEAS!*> *A* girl shouts out.

<*FRYING PAN'S GOT THE FLEAS......*>

* * *

That funny looking yellow coin

After raiding my dad's pockets for any lose change, I legged it out of that house and made my way to school via Sid's Sweetshop.

My siblings and I were supposed to walk the route together - As far as our parents were concerned, all three of us walked hand-in-hand like half of the Von-Trapp family.

Truth be told, the older siblings didn't want to walk with me and nor did I (want to walk with them), that way I could nip into Sid's and buy sweets for myself...only!

The way I saw it, raiding dad's pockets in the morning had risks. As I was the only one willing to covertly enter their bedroom, I should be the only one to enjoy the bounty.

This may explain why, by the time I reached ten, I had half a dozen fillings in my teeth!

Once at the sweetshop, I pulled out the handful of coins and took a look at them.

Good. New coins. Five pence coins and a ten pence. None of those old threepence or sixpence and chiefly no old pennies... except this odd looking heavy yellow one with an old man's face.

I stuck the odd looking (*probably Greek*) coin in my pocket and with a hand held out, palm up, coins in the middle, I thrust my hand towards Sid (the main man) and demanded <*SWEETS!*>

Back at school, in the playground just before the first bell, I met up with my (new) best friend (the old one acted like a right bastard when he found out I had nits) and offered him a handful of Pear Drops, making sure the bastard witnessed my generosity.

New best buddy brought in some football cards and we agreed to an exchange or sale if I had nothing to exchange with.
I pulled out of my pocket some change left over from Sid's and offered seven pence for Frank McLintock, George Graham and Pat Rice football cards. Charlie George's card would have been seven pence on its own.
New best friend spots the foreign looking coin I fished out with the other money and says <*my dad collects old coins, I swap yer for Bob Wilson.*>
<*Naa, it's a Greek coin so I want more cards,*> I said with my best poker face.
<I*t's Bob Wilson man....best goalie...ever*!>
<*Ok Bob Wilson and Steve Perryman.*> Best buddy offers.
<*Get lost – Steve Perryman is Tottenham and they are shit...really shit, the shittest team in London,*> I may have said.
In the end, my persistence paid off and I swapped the old coin for the original three cards and saved myself the seven pence. The day was going to turn out ok ...for once.

I was sat in the back of the classroom colouring in a new masterpiece I had just sketched. It was almost playtime and the class was getting restless. I was just about to sneak another Pear Drop in my gob when my ex friend calls out from the front of the class <*Frying Pan, IS THAT YOUR MUM?*>
Although I heard the little shit, his words did not comprehend, I didn't understand..... *What would my mum be doing here?*
I wasn't going to move, but he said it again and so did some other kid who knew what my mum looked like.

I got up, walked towards the front and there she was, looking through the rectangular window set into the door. It was a small window and her head filled most of it. She had that look, the look prior to calling out the devil in Greek. The look that comes before a beating. Then again maybe I got the look wrong, maybe she was here to ....NO, it's definitely a beating, she just put her fist to her mouth and bit it!

The teacher noticed her and went to see what she wanted. There was a brief conversation by the door. Actually there was no conversation. The teacher was trying to have a dialogue and my mum was trying to get past her to me.
The teacher motioned for her to wait outside in the hallway and closed the door behind her. She then turned and instructed me to leave the class to talk to my mother.
The whole class stopped what they were doing. They all saw me stand and walk slowly around the desks with hunched shoulders and head down. They noticed that I was avoiding eye contact. They all saw that no sooner had I opened the door, a hand appeared and grabbed me by the hair.
They heard a slap and they heard me cry out *<WHAT HAVE I DONE NOW?>*
I heard the whole class gasp in surprise, then laugh in hysterics. There's nothing more amusing than watching a kid from school getting smacked by his mum and there's nothing more embarrassing either!
And you wonder why I'm sociably (not socially) awkward...

Turns out, that the funny yellow coin was a small gold sovereign coin, twenty-two carats and that old man's face was King George V. –worth a few hundred today so fuck knows what the equivalent was back then.
You'd be happy to hear that I got the coin back, but only after I gave all the football cards back, as well as the rest of my change and the last of my Pear Drops....along with the threat that I would bash-him-up if he didn't agree to the swap.
As you will find out from a later chapter – this episode did not stop me from venturing into my dad's pockets. Something far more terrifying than a beating would stop me that's for sure.

* * *

Charlie George and The Arsenal.

Charlie George, superstar, he walks like a woman and he wears a bra....
Obviously I am an Arsenal fan.
They say you never forget the day when you choose to follow a team and for me that day was one Saturday morning in May 1971.
I was out shopping with my mother. Every Saturday morning she would take one of us out to help with the bags, or translate if the need arose, or perhaps she just wanted company.
The others would stay behind and look after the baby siblings.
This particular week was my turn. We left our house and headed towards the Holloway Road. I started noticing a few bods with red and white scarfs around their neck and a few tied round their wrists. Then as we approached the market on route

to Safeway's, the market stall holders were wearing rosettes, large ones with red and white ribbons and some with a large picture of a cannon in the middle.
(*I'm getting goose pimples as I write this*).
I noticed the flags on poles sticking out the top of the stalls. Some read A.F.C and others ARSENAL. The place was buzzing. The talk was about the Arsenal v Liverpool F.A Cup final and how "we" are going to win 3-1 and bring the cup back home. ("We"... false-of-habit. You see... I have used inverted commas).
I could have stood there all day soaking up the atmosphere.

I played football (well, I kicked a ball when I eventually beat all the other kids to it) in the school playground.
I knew of the Arsenal as well as the other top teams of that decade thanks to football cards you found in Lucky Bags, but I never really supported or followed any team's progress. However I did know even back then, that Tottenham Hotspur were shit....I mean really shit. Crap then as they are today.
Seeing the Holloway Road covered in red and white triggered a feeling within me, a passion, a wanting to belong sensation. The hairs on the back of my scrawny neck stood on end and had I had pubic hairs, they would have stood on end too.
The stall at the end row was selling Arsenal rosettes. I had to have one. I had to wear the badge to identify myself as one of them. I want to be an Arsenal Fan – I am an Arsenal Fan.......and I begged my mum to buy me one.

The guy on the market stall patted my head and then wiped his hand on his trouser leg. As he pinned the Arsenal Rosette onto my t-shirt, we had the following conversation...
<*What do you think of Tottenham*?> He asks.
<*Shit.*> Was my reply.
<*What do you think of shit*?> He asks again.
<*Tottenham.*> I shout out.
<*Thank you son.*> He says.
<*That's alright.*> I say
And as I walked away, I heard him singing...<*We hate Tottenham, we hate Tottenham....*>
My understanding is that the conversation between the market stall holder and myself became a famous chant at Highbury – the home of The Arsenal.
My mother and I were just about to exit the market, when the market stall holder shouts out, <*don't forget the game is on the goggle-box later....*>

I had to get home, I had to watch the game. That shopping trip was the longest ever, but made sufferable with my large red and white Arsenal rosette pinned proudly to my chest.

I'd be lying if I said I was engrossed with my first live (on TV) football game. It dragged on a bit to be honest, especially as there were no goals (meaning the game went into extra time). The fact that the black and white picture kept jumping whenever somebody walked past the TV with an indoor aerial placed on top (which was practically every ten minutes),

proved how much of a Gooner (one who supports the Arsenal Gunners) I wanted to be.
And I was dying for a piss!!
Turns out I wanted to go number twos too.
Extra time was about to start, so I turned up the TV volume and ran to the toilet.
I missed the first two goals due to a flipping turtle head.
In the end, I had to wipe several times before I could run back in and as luck would have it - just in time to see Charlie George toe-punt the ball in the back of the net.
Can I suggest for the few who have not seen Charlie George's F.A Cup winner, to Youtube "Charlie George F.A Cup 1971" because my description will not do it justice.
I just wish I had Youtube or indeed the internet when I was young, then I would not have had to rely on my big brother describing Chesty Morgan!

Charlie George scores the winner of the 1971 F.A cup. He runs towards the half way line, slides down on both knees and then proceeds to lie down on his back. All the other Arsenal players run towards him, hoist him up, embrace and pat him on the back like the Arsenal hero he is.

The following Monday at school, during lunch time, we somehow managed to arrange a fifty-a-side football game. In reality it was more like seventy-thirty as most kids wanted to be Arsenal. We only had one goal and that was the side of the caretaker's shed.

It was total mayhem. There were no goalies, no defenders or midfielders....everyone wanted to be a striker. So once again, a hundred kids chasing down one ball.
Call it fate, or destiny, but I just happen to be taking a rest by the shed (passive smoker's lungs) when the ball rolls towards me. With the instincts and reflexes of a hungry Holloway cat I turn and shoot and ....GOAL!!!!!
The ball hits the shed with a thud.
Finally, this could be my turning point, my Charlie George moment.
<*GOALLLLLLLL.*> I shout and run excitedly like that same Holloway cat with a firework (that somebody) tied to its tail.
I run to the centre of the playground. I refrain from sliding on my knees as this is an Inner City school – all concrete and no grass. I lay on my back with my arms stretched out waiting for the sixty-nine kids on my team to heave me up.
With arms stretched out, I still await some of my team to come to me. With tired arms and a tilt of my head to see what's keeping my team, I await to be hoisted up. I might as well wait all bloody day.
The game restarted the moment the ball rebounded off the shed wall.
I get up, dust myself down and pray that nobody noticed.

* * *

Old McDonald's...

According to Google, the first McDonald's restaurant to open in the UK was in South East London in November 1974.
That makes me eleven years of age and in the last year of primary school. So by my reckoning, the second (or close third) McDonald's to open shortly after, was the one in Holloway (Seven Sisters Road to be exact).

The back of this restaurant backed onto our playground at the rear of our school. Our playground was fifty-two metres by thirty-two metres of pure building foundation poured concrete, most likely reinforced with granite. When you fell over during kiss-chase, you flipping felt it!
When I broke my arm on that bastard, it took months to heal and to this day I still cannot straighten it at the elbow.
To give our playground that realistic prison yard look, the play area was closed in by a four metres high steel chain linked fence. Had the school budget not been reduced during construction, they would have topped it with razor wire.
Regardless of the penitentiary feel, we still had ourselves some pretty good playtimes. None more so than the day we delayed the opening of the second (or close third) McDonald's restaurant to open in the UK.

Construction works were well underway on the new restaurant and all building materials and machinery were laid out in the Mews, rear of the site – which happened to be in full view of the playground.

For months, those inconsiderate builders were making one hell of a racket and we kids during our break and lunch times couldn't hear ourselves scream!
The only person happy with the works going on was a substitute teacher from the United States who told us that when the place called McDonald's opened, our parents (or parole officer) would be able to buy us a hamburger and milkshake for under 50p. (Yeah, I can see my dad leaving his steakhouse to buy me a hamburger). The excited substitute teacher then tried to describe a Big Mac, but we lost interest and went back to our game.

One day at morning break time we rushed out into the playground like escaped lunatics. Suddenly we stopped in our tracks. Our view into the Mews, where we lined up along the chain fence to abuse baldy men with shouts of <*Hey Baldy,*> was obstructed with the builders' materials and fixtures.
They'd gone and lined up along the whole width of our fence (to keep off the narrow road most likely) large items such as galvanised steel ventilation ducting, expensive looking industrial chrome cooker hoods, chrome splashbacks, a large M-sign and many other fittings that looked custom-built for Mac's.
This was going too far. We had put up with the mess and noise and dust, but encroaching onto our space and blocking out our south view of the outside world – well this was a bloody liberty.
It must be the cockney in us. That old "look after our manor" ethos. By the end of break, we had devised a course of action –

if successful it would get us back our view and stick one back to the builders by the end of lunchtime.

When I say “we” I must admit the plan was mine.
We had a quick lunch. Well most of us did. A few stayed behind when the dinner lady announced there was second puddings. The call for second dinners and/or second puddings was met with a stampede. Especially by those on free-dinners.
For those of you who don’t know, or were fortunate to go to an outer London primary school with green fields and not ballast riddled concrete for football pitches, the call for second dinners was normally on a Friday when the dinner lady was left with extra portions of fish fingers or jam roly-poly. Rather than binning them, she would offer the remains to the kids. Actually, she offered the left-overs to the fast skinny kids who were able to bolt out of the traps like Greyhounds. We slower kids with Rickets could never make it to the food counter in time. Ok slight exaggeration with the Rickets thing....but we poor kids need all the sympathy going.

Once out in the playground, we separated into two groups. One group headed for the east end netball pole and my group headed for the west.
The iron netball poles were sixty-five millimetres in diameter, standing at nine foot tall with another two feet set in the steel holes cemented into the ground. We all tried to get a grip around the poles and ended up head-butting each other. So then we nominated three of the fatter kids (who are generally stronger than skinny kids at that age) to grasp the pole and lift

with all their chubby might. Once the pole moved up a foot, another three kids would grab further down the bottom. All six kids would lift and strain till the rapturous noise of farts and then cheers would sound when the pole was lifted clear of the hole. Then it tilted and crashed to the ground.
You younger readers are now asking - <*Where were the mealtime supervisors?*>
My reply is – <*The what?*>

Thirty seconds later, we heard the other pole smash to the floor. Then bounce up a foot, and clatter back down.
Fifteen seconds later both teams, with half a dozen kids either end of both poles, marched up to the south end of the playground like medieval warriors about to storm a castle armed with two long and awesome battering rams. The girls were following cheering on their champions.

The objective was simple. Run, ram and smash into the fence to knock down as many of the offending items stacked by our fence before the builders come back from their lunch.
The noise was incredible. It sounded like Mike Oldfield's Tubular Bells. The expensive looking chrome cooker hoods made the most noise. First they absorbed the pole's impact with a bass harmonic and then it struck the floor with mid-level and treble vibes. I would take a guess that there was an octave change with that dent in that hood.
The flat chrome splashbacks sounded like an orchestra's cymbals finale. Sshshshhhhhshshshsh followed by the

crash....and the then the climax of the large plastic yellow M sign.
As it happens, it was a bit of an anti-climax because it fell and just cracked – no smash!
The thunderous noise brought on roars of cheers from the rest of the playground. It also woke up some teachers from their stupor. I would also hazard a guess that the noise was heard at the greasy spoon because one minute after our standing ovation, the playground scattered as teachers and builders arrived from different directions.
The teachers entered through the gate from the school building. Two of the builders tried to force open the steel fire exit gates built into the steel fencing.
Upon seeing two large burly Irishmen trying to squeeze through the gap between the two gates, my buddies and I decided to take refuge behind the teachers. After all, a clip round the ear-o is better than an Irishman's shovel up your arse.
I ask you. What kind of beefy idiot attempts to chase an eleven year old around a school playground?
Rickets or not – it was like someone shouting <SECOND DINNERS!>

A month later, cards were posted through neighbouring letterboxes, including my street. The cards invited you for a free McDonald's burger and fries or burger and milkshake at the newly opened McDonald's restaurant.
I'm embarrassed to say, but eating your first MacD's hamburger is comparable to people asking where you were

when Kennedy was shot. I was almost two months old so I was at home!

CHAPTER 10A:-MY FIRST TRIP TO HIGHBURY STADIUM (RE-WRITE)

Five months after my Charlie George antics, my favourite uncle took me to my first Arsenal match at the Highbury Stadium.

I've have had to re-write this chapter because my description of that day, my feelings and emotions were in parts, similar to Nick Hornby's Fever Pitch. I didn't want to get done for plagiarism, so one thousand words were removed. Shame because, those one thousand words were the best I have ever written. I captured the emotion of seeing the bright green pitch with passion and intensity. Now my word-count has been reduced, so I have to make up the word tally by waffling.

My favourite uncle is my mother's younger brother who lived only five minutes from our house. My mother took me round to my uncles one Saturday for a visit and to deliver some Greek food, as she had made too much for the restaurant.
He was a proud uncle when he heard that I discovered Arsenal all by myself. He asked me if I wanted to go to the football with him.
<*What football?*> I asked.
<*Arsenal, who else?*> My uncle says.
<*Where do they play, is it far?*> I asked.

<*Highbury is just up the road. A ten minute walk.*>
I had no concept of geography but I was good at sums.
<*You mean to say that I only live a twenty minute walk from Arsenal?*> I asked.
<*Fifteen minutes.*> My uncle corrects.
I told you that I'm going to waffle for a thousand words!
<*Why didn't anybody tell me?*>
<*Do you want to go or what?*> Uncle was getting impatient.
<*Does Chesty Morgan have big tits?*> I said <*Of course I want to go.*>
I was advanced for my age thanks to big brother, but I may have remembered the conversation differently.
<*When?*> I asked
<*This afternoon... in two hours' time.*>
<*IN TWO HOURS' TIME???*> I screamed excitedly. Then I started dancing what can only be described as a Greek-Irish fusion jig!

Two hours later, my uncle and I set off for the match.
<*You can stop dancing now, unless you want to be beaten up by the Newcastle fans,*> my uncle says.
<*Are Arsenal playing Newcastle?*>
We turned into the Hornsey Road and were met with a sea of red and white. Hundreds of men and boys with red and white scarfs around their necks or in their hands. When we turned into Drayton Park, there were thousands of fans, all walking in the same direction as us. The nearer we got to the stadium, the louder the chanting became.
"*Good old Arsenal,*
We're proud to say that name,
While we sing this song, we'll win the game!"

While some fans continued straight, others turned into a residential road and we followed.

I have to admit, this didn't seem a likely place for a football stadium. The crowds were packed into a small narrow side street. There were stalls selling scarfs and match programmes but no sign of a football stadium. I was just about to ask my uncle if we were heading in the right direction, when I saw a white concrete building with red windows just after a row of houses. We had arrived at the most famous sports ground in the world – belonging to the most famous football team in the world. But my initial reaction was <*is this it*?>

The place was deafening, with various songs and renditions, all containing the word "Arsenal."

My uncle takes hold of my arm and leads me off the road onto the footpath and tells me we are to wait here. He had arranged to meet a work colleague at their usual waiting spot and a few minutes later, his mate arrived with his two sons.

I was introduced to the boys. One was my age and the other was slightly younger.

<*Is this your first time*?> I asked the kid my age.

<*More like my one-hundredth.*> He replies with a smugness that suggested he was really a Spurs fan!

It turns out my assumption was wrong. He really was an Arsenal fan. Six years later, I found out from my uncle that this kid was arrested for hooliganism outside Finsbury Park Station.

<*Lets go.*> My uncle's work colleague says and we all follow him around the ground to a set of turnstiles.

<*Where are we sitting uncle*?> I had to shout to be heard above the chanting of "Ar-sen-al, Ar-sen-al."
<*Sitting*?> The older brother questions.
<We're not sitting.> My uncle says. <*We stand behind the goal….*>
<*At the North-Bank*,> says the future hooligan. Then joins in the chorus of "Ar-sen-al, Ar-sen-al."
<*We are not standing at the North-Bank.*> His dad says to boos from his kids.
<*We stand at the Clock-End.*> My uncle says.
<*I'll be at the North-Bank when I'm older.*> Says the future hooligan.
The colleague pays the guy by the window who presses a button. This allows him and his kids to push through the turnstile one at a time. My uncle pays for our admission with mine costing around fifty pence, which is a bit of a rip-off, but it is The Arsenal after all.
No surprise, I struggled to master the turnstile by pushing it the wrong way!
We enter the ground and make our way to the stairs leading to the stands.
For my true feelings from this point, I suggest you watch (or read) Nick Hornby's Fever Pitch. In the meantime, I'll waffle to the end of the chapter…….

Emanating from the darkness, I walked out to a stadium illumined by a bright afternoon sun. The stars life-giving rays radiate off the greenest grass found only in the Garden of Eden.

The reverberation of sounds echoing around the stadium, is resounding and welcoming as the warmth from a Gregorian chant is to its spiritual masses.
I raise my arms in splendour as I slowly rotate to absorb the ecclesiastical house of worship.
My eyes capture the cyclical colours of red and white. Instantly, I am reminded of Vincent Van Gogh's masterpiece- Vase with Red Poppies.
I look to the heavens and I hear God's whispers. "Anyone who hears these words of mine and obeys them is like a wise man who built his house on rock." This place is a house on a rock and the Arsenal's manager Bertie Mee's words will lead the team to salvation.
As I lower myself in thanks and prayer, I am told to get out the fucking way as I am blocking the way!

And as it happens – I have made up the one thousand words!

CHAPTER 11:-PAKEMAN STREET II. PLAYING OUT AND OTHER ADVENTURES

There was a primary school in Pakeman Street but I didn't go to it as mum fell out with an auntie who lived literally next door to Pakeman School. Instead of going to a primary school nearby with our cousins, mum enrolled me and my siblings up at another school, which meant that on my way home I would have to run the gauntlet walking home to Pakeman Street, whilst avoiding the hoodlums coming out of Pakeman School. We moved to Pakeman Street during my final years at primary school and a year later I would go to secondary school with the same hoodlums. So twelve months or so of intimidation and bullying were chalked up to life skills training, which was invaluable for anybody thinking of going to my secondary school.

During the first years at the new house, the only time I would see my dad would be when I went to the restaurant in the evening to help big brother clean up and to take whatever homemade Greek Cypriot dishes my mother cooked for the patrons. I tell a lie, I would see part of him for the odd minute in the morning when he would be sleeping and I would sneak in and "borrow" a sixpence or whatever small change he happened to have in the small pocket within his side pocket of his suit jacket. I would sneak in most mornings for my pocket money owed, even after I mistakenly took a funny looking yellow coin and nearly died in my mum's hands the afternoon that followed.

I did eventually stop going into their room in the mornings. You would too having seen what I'd seen. That day I sneaked in and caused my dad to roll off the top of mum – both stark flipping naked.

<What in Roger Moore's name were they playing at? - make your effing minds up parents.>

It wasn't his swearing that shit me up, although he did throw out some classic Cypriot curses about screwing my maternal heritage. No, what shit me up and burnt my retinas was the sight of his naked arse. If only he did not roll off to chase me out.....the sight of his penis was ghastly and life changing for a pubescent teen!

Still parents rolling about in the brambles was better than parents fighting at four in the morning. Shame they couldn't stick to rolling around in the hay instead of involving us in their shit and driving us mad.

I don't want to dwell on my parents' sex life, I mean what person would. But it is something that needs to be said so that I can try and get my head around their relationship.

We kids thought moving to this big house with new and large bits of furniture would usher a new era of family life. Sadly apart from the odd act of lust that overcame them once in a while, their behaviour always reverted to arguing, then shouting, followed by swearing, fighting, hitting and

screaming. I think we older kids were immune to it. Cannot say the same for the younger siblings I'm afraid.
For me, I found a way to escape home turmoil and that was to hang about outside the house – all hours if possible.

Pakeman Street was a great place to hang about and play in the streets after school. Nowadays, this would be called unsocial behaviour and the whole street would be on ASBOs – Anti Social Behaviour Orders - but I ask you, what is anti-social about kicking a ball in the street or making a ruckus by shouting and screaming and laughing while the old boys indoors are trying to read The Evening Standard in their front rooms?
Nope, playing outside in the street took you away from any home issues and gave you the freedom to run around like an idiot. Outside, you had your buddies and the streets and no end of pranks to play. You felt safe...........safe until somebody in the next street would shout...
<THE DOONIGANS – THE DOONIGANS ARE COMING....>

* * *

The Doonigans. The Doonigans are coming.

You never saw a street empty so quickly.
Kids would run in all directions and god help you if you came out and didn't put your front door on the latch! Kids would be

banging on doors, bikes would be dragged into front gardens and hidden behind front gardens' walls. You'd be begging somebody on the inside to hurry up and open the door because THE DOONIGANS ARE COMING!
Mothers would run outside after hearing the commotion and drag the little ones who had no concept of what a Doonigan was. Any boy scouts washing cars for Bob-a-Job week would abandon their watery soapy buckets and sponges and leg it out of Pakeman street. Not that we had any hookers, but if we did, then they too would take off with knickers around their ankles leaving punters to fend off The Doonigans with bribes of fags.

So forty-seven seconds after the first shout, the whole street would be abandoned, deserted of all life. The only movement would be discarded sweet wrappers picked up by the wind, rolled together and sent onwards like a tumbleweed being blown down the middle of Pakeman Street towards the junction of Mayton Street. Doors that were left on latches would be slamming against the frame and the knocker on that door would bang out like a death bell, announcing the arrival of death themselves – The Doonigans.
From behind twitching curtains you would see them round the corner...and there, by the school gates on the corner, a Doonigan.
...and another, and another....
There were nine Doonigans in total. Where one travelled, they all travelled. No single Doonigan was ever seen alone. In fact, nobody knew anything about them. Where they went to school, where they lived, their names (except the surname –

Doonigan). To be honest, nobody could tell you who the first person was to find out that their surname was Doonigan. All that anybody knew was, when you saw a Doonigan, you run. If you heard the shout <Doonigan>, you shit yourself, then run. The stories told about the Doonigans would have been horrific. But there were no stories – only that you run!
Perhaps the reason there were no tales of Doonigan transgressions was that people were good at running.
I never saw a ghost, but I was shit-scared of ghosts, just like me and the whole neighbourhood were shit-scared of The Doonigans!

The rest is all conjecture and observations from a safe distance......

The eldest was a boy of around nineteen. He was tall, wiry, and sinewy-built with a glue-sniffing philtrum (the curved bit of the top lip, under the nose).
If you have not had the chance to mingle with or run away from glue-sniffers, allow me to give you a quick brief. But first, I just want to say that I was never into glue-sniffing. I did accidently sniff when I was making Airfix models or hammer House of Horror monster figurines, but never sought a buzz form Evo-Stick. For those who did partake, along with the spaced out vacant look, their top lip would become dry and cracked and the philtrum would look shrivelled. They would have this snarling look where the top lip is pulled up due to the glue's reaction to the skin – hence glue-sniffing top lip.
Obviously, not backed by medical research, just my observations.

The youngest Doonigan was a boy of roughly five years of age and in-between the youngest and oldest, there were a further three boys ranging from ten to fifteen. There were also four girls aged approximately twelve to eighteen.
The rest of the boys were smaller versions of the eldest including the scabby top lip but with decreasing severity as the Doonigan got younger.
The eldest looking girl had boobs to rival Chesty Morgan's, but the Doonigan's hung lower due to the bra-less look of the 1970s. She too had the glue-sniffing lip, but brightened up with a bit of Twiggy red lipstick by Maxfactor.
They walked in order, oldest boy, oldest girl, boy, girl, girl and so on till you got to Jimmy Osmond Doonigan.
They walked with a purpose whilst twitching and smoking. They all smoked, even the Long Haired Lover from Liverpool, and in the back pocket of the older boy would be the brown paper bag with the damp glue patch.
They held their lit cigarettes curled up in their palms and when they smoked they would raise their clasped fists to their mouths and pull the longest drag possible and then their top lips curled and the snarl would appear.

Shit!! My elbow slipped off the window seal. The curtain moved – shit. All the Doonigans looked towards my house simultaneously. I dared not move. I dared not breathe. I took a step back. I held my breath. If my mum came now with the broom, I still wouldn't have moved.

Pakeman Street is eighty-seven metres long. I did the maths. The average person walks 1.4m/s. So from the time the first Doonigan was spotted, it would take him sixty-two seconds to exit our road. Then there were the other eight all walking at the same speed, at a distance of one metre apart. A further eight seconds. Then the little one dropped his fag – add seven more seconds for him to pick it off the floor and put it back in his mouth.

The longest, almost one and a half minutes was over, as the littlest Doonigan head disappeared from view.
Curtains started twitching and slowly, the bravest of us were the first to open their doors.
I went outside and met up with the others. That was close we would say...and then exchange stories of how the Doonigans smashed bottles and scratched cars and picked on the old man walking his dog and how one nearly caught me, but I shook him off as I ran towards the corner shop and back, going the long way around the block.
We would then warn all the youngsters to avoid the Doonigans at all costs!

* * *

Crap22

Any similarities to Oliver Stone's 1986 Vietnam Movie Platoon is purely coincidental ... if anything, I should own the rights to a particular scene!

You may not remember the movie Platoon, but you might remember the movie poster where a young Willem Dafoe is on his knees with arms stretched up in the air – shot in the back – staring up to the heavens in bewilderment and sorrow.

In the movie, they played the sad theme tune "Adagio for Strings" which had your pubic hairs standing on end. Man that scene was powerful.

Anyway – Holloway in the seventies was full of dog-shit. Wherever you went, there were turds the size of Cypriot watermelons on every kerbstone and footpath. Some occupied two kerbstones or paving slabs - they were so big.

Today you would need a Tesco bag for life to carry that crap off to the nearest wheelie bin.

So there we were, young foolish and bored. There's three of us tonight with bangers in our pockets and mischief on our minds. We are wandering around Mayton Street, just around the corner from Pakeman Street, following the golden rule - never shit on your doorstep, which tonight had a literal connotation.

As always, it was my idea...they were always my ideas.

I spotted the old landlord's nearly new Rover 2000 in metallic brown parked near the one-bed-sleeps-seven flat and a quick flashback to that fucked up Ascot water heater made up my mind. Time to get even.

I just finished a packet of salt & vinegar. I pulled out two of my ice-lolly sticks from my back pocket and my buddies and I went in search of the brown stuff.
Now you are asking, what I was doing with ice-lolly sticks in my back pocket. Well my friendly modern day reader of kindles, this was the seventies and we were poor. We played with ice-lolly sticks the same way we played conkers, or in your case - Nintendo DS.
One of us would hold out his ice-lolly stick horizontally between both hands and the other guy would whack the centre with his stick. You would hold your attacking stick like a knife and come down quick and hard like a karate chop, and if you cracked or went through your opponent's stick, your stick would win and become a one-er. Or if you broke two sticks consecutively – a two-er and so on.
Please don't ask <*what are conkers?*>

No sooner than we set off, we almost trod in the stuff. There on the floor was a Mr Whippy turd, long and spiralled to a tip. You can just imagine the dog's arse rotating and swivelling like he has a hula-hoop round his hips producing that Mr Whippy shaped turd.
I carefully bent down and scooped up the stinky stuff with the ice-lolly sticks and whilst balancing the shit on the sticks, I placed it into the empty crisp bag. I looked up at my friend and motioned to his half empty smoky bacon flavoured crisps and told him to hurry up and finish off the packet cause we are gonna need another bag!

We moved on and only twenty-five feet later, we came across another lump of shit. This dog had sweetcorn last night!
Naah only kidding – thought it was a funny thing to say – made me laugh to myself (insert L, O and another L).

This turd was half on the kerb and half onto the carriageway. A tricky one to get into the bag. But between the three of us, we managed with minimal shit on our finger tips.
With the state of our fingernails, you wouldn't have noticed anyway. I had long pink nails and on the ends (google says the white bits are called the distal edge of the fingernail), well the 5mm distal edge was black with under nail muck. Not proud of it, just trying to give a full description of events!
Fifteen minutes later, with Mayton Street cleared of its dog shit, we had two empty crisp bags now full of shit – filled to the brim. And this was the 1970s- crisps bags hadn't shrunk to the micro packets you guys have today (sorry if I assuming all the readers are younger than me. It makes me feel superior and arrogant if I hold this belief).

Back to the landlord's Rover we traipsed, arms held out in front holding out the two bags with thumb and index finger straining under the weight. Our woolly jumper necks over our noses in a poor attempt to filter out any shit air particles.
It was a dark winter's evening and we had the streets to ourselves.
Careful not to rip the bags, we emptied the shitty contents on the pavement beside the ex-landlord's car. Then we scraped out the remaining sticky stuff, like one would clean a jar of

peanut butter. We managed to get all the dogs' mess out onto a good sized pile beside the car. For good measure, I cleaned off the lolly-sticks by wiping them on all four of the Rover's door handles.
(Yep, I know, I know – what an utter ~~~~ I am).

Right, here's the rest of the plan.
I placed two bangers (fireworks – short fuse, loud bang variety) into the middle of the dog shit pile and twisted both fuses together.
One thing for Holloway is that you can buy fireworks months before and after Guy Fawkes Night and there was no age limitations. A five year old could buy cigarettes and a bottle of whiskey if you couldn't be bothered to go yourself and you happened to have a younger brother that would go for you!

I got the matches out and we all readied ourselves for a sprint. The idea was simple, light the fuse, run like a bastard, get to a safe distance, turn around and BANG! Watch the dog shit explode all over the metallic brown Rover........just a shame it wasn't white (the car that is, not the dog shit. Although... we did come across white dog shit, but they were too solid, thus would not have splattered on impact. Most likely, the white dog shit would have smashed the car's windscreen).
I struck a match and lit the fuse...
My friends got off no sooner than I pulled the Swannie out the box (Swannie – Swan Vesta matches, the red tip ones that you can strike on the ground or on the bodywork of a Rover 2000 and it would ignite).

Because I twisted the blue paper fuses together, it seemed to have shortened the length of the fuse and the time to lift off. The damn thing lit in the middle...
I had seconds to leg it...
I legged it.........then slipped and tripped forwards on my hands and knees. I tried to get up off my knees and put some distance between me and the ca.............BANG!
I fell back down on my knees. *<I'm hit....I'M HIT.>*
I heard a wet splat-splat sound.
My back was getting peppered with shit-shots.
One small lump hit the back of my head. I had my new parker coat on and had it not been for the fur rim around the hood, my neck would have been covered in poo.
I screamed and held up my arms to the gods.
My ears were ringing and my nose was sniffing-in dog shit and gunpowder cocktails.
I looked up in misapprehension...and sorrow.
I heard a sad acoustic guitar solo. It could have been Adagio for Strings. Correction- it was Mud's Tiger-Feet playing out of a window nearby.
<Why god?> I shouted.........*<Why me?>*......then BANG!
Shit! Forgot about the second one!

* * *

Stink Bombs

Stink bombs came in fragile glass vials and stunk of rotten eggs and military grade farts when the fragile little bottle shaped container broke and the liquid was exposed to air.
They were sold for use as pranks and although they were funny then, I humbly apologise to that West-Indian family that we forced to evacuate from their house one evening.
If the guy gave us our ball back last week, we wouldn't have picked his house.
We (I was never alone. One had to be egged on, excuse the pun) lifted up the letterbox cover and threw a stink bomb inside the hallway. It didn't break. So the next one we broke off the top of the vial and poured the liquid inside the letterbox.
We ran to the corner and hid behind a car to see what effect the stink bomb would have.
It was a warm summer's evening, almost dusk and visibility was good. I managed to get some of the stink bomb on my fingers. If two drops smelt awful and had me choking, it wouldn't be long till someone came out that house shouting blue murder. It was the plan after all, to evoke a reaction for our callous, sick sense of fun. But the response that followed was beyond what we expected.
I thought it was funny then, but now as I write this, I have to admit I'm slightly embarrassed. Still, let's continue. After all, these are true events and an insight into how some would act to escape from one type of madness to another.
Out of the house they came, one after the other. First came the mother who was in a very large dressing gown covering a very large body and had done something to her afro hair.

To us, it looked like worms on her head, but now I understand it's an afro hair night-time care procedure.
Then daughter number one, dressed and looking the same as her mother, followed. As did daughter number two and three, all in dressing gowns and all in readiness for an early night or just a normal pre-bed ritual.
I hate to say that we found this amusing.
The women of the house were holding their noses and shouting out for Jesus.
Two young boys came running out next, dressed in pyjamas.
Holy shit, this was working out better than we thought as we patted each other on the back....
Last out was the dad. A big man. A builder with wide shoulders and big hands. He came out with is trademark Trilby hat and he looked pissed.
We were giggling at the scene unfolding before us and then we noticed the cricket bat...........and he noticed us.
<RUN!>

Why did we deviate from our normal venue for letting off stink bombs? – Namely, Holloway tube station.
We would wait at the beginning of the platform and when the tube doors were about to close in on the cramped passengers, we would chuck in as many stink bombs as possible before the doors could fully close. Then we would run up towards the end of the platform watching the train pass with all the poor sods stuck on an underground train, in summer, stuffed like sardines in a tin - gasping for any fresh air their lungs could

syphon through their windpipe, without choking on the stench of ammonium sulphide – aka stink bombs.

No, that night we broke a cardinal rule and shat on our doorstep!
The guy with the cricket bat took off after us and for a big guy, he initially had speed. I couldn't help notice his red eyes and thought – *wow he's really pissed.*
He was calling out after us and shouting about our "bloodclarts" (whatever they are) and then something about ruining his buzz and if he caught us he would chop our bollocks off...man!
I think he could have caught us, especially with that lightening start he got when he spotted us. But by the time he reached the corner we were hiding behind, he seemed to have lost interest. We however continued to run and looked behind us at every opportunity, but the big guy just stood there on the corner we had just vacated. He seemed to be playing cricket, by taking up a stance ready to hit a fast ball bowled by an invisible entity, then swinging at the imaginary ball, which I assumed he took for one of our heads.
He must have breathed in too much stink bomb gas – because he looked way out of it!

That night we stayed out and away from our yard longer than I had wanted, so one way or another, when I eventually made it home, I'd definitely got beats from something made of wood. Still, could have been worse!

CHAPTER 12:-A BOYS ONLY SECONDARY SCHOOL IN HOLLOWAY.

Charlie George went to my school.
I should end this chapter now whilst the going is good. Finish it on a high and not mention any bad stuff just in case OFSTED decide to sue me. But a quick internet search of my old school showed that it is no longer a boy's only school, but a successful mixed school with no reports of arson, kidnappings, sex scandals, vandalism or any mindless act of violence.

The first time I heard the shout <*fight*> was only three days into the new term. The shout was heard from the rear playground known to pupils as The Gambling Pitch, where dinner money was won and lost. The concrete ground had five-a-side football pitch line markings, which made it ideal for penny up the wall, penny near the line and so on – but played without pennies as the minimum buy-in was ten pence.

I followed the stampede of boys into The Gambling Pitch and was met by a hundred strong circle of boys, jeering and cheering the two fighters in the centre.
It sounded brutal. I had to see this fight, to see how big boys fought, to see if the headlock was being used. So being a first year and small, I made my way through the throng of larger boys towards the centre. I pushed and snuck and went under

legs, twisted and turned and finally made my way to the front. I was scared and squinted to block out some of the violence that I was about to witness. And what I witnessed was brutal in an unexpected way.

At first I couldn't comprehend what I was seeing. My mind was having trouble decoding the data. Similar to catching your parents at it. You stare even though you're aware what you are seeing is wrong but not recognising what is wrong.

On reaching the front of the circle, there in the middle of the battle arena were two of the music teachers from the music block. They were slapping and girly-punching and attempting shin high kicks and helicopter punches.

I stood there, with head tilted to the side, confused. This never happened at my old primary school. What have I let myself in for? Not that I had a choice. After my shameful fight with a girl at primary school, there was no way I'd be allowed to go to a mixed secondary school.

There were shouts of <go *on sir – chin-im*> from the crowd of older kids and a look of bewilderment from the younger ones.

I decided to move away from the action when I saw some of the older kids throw the odd punch at the lame fighters. I knew that it wouldn't be long till the big kids would, in frustration of not hitting a teacher, aim one of their punches at someone smaller. And I was right!

It was a welcomed introduction to big school.

Now I knew I had to be ready for anything as the rules were different here. I needed to fit in and fit in quick or look to avoid incidents.

As it happened, two days later, I got into a fight which proved pivotal to surviving the secondary school years. Pivotal and obstructive as I then had to live up to my new nickname.....
I got the nickname Psycho-Pan.

Psycho

I was a week into secondary school and unlike some of the other new kids, I had yet to be singled out for a beating or parted from my dinner money. Natural survival instincts were triggered in many of the first year pupils and they sought protection by swimming together like herrings in large schools forming one large group. But like nature, the slower ones were being picked off the ends.
It was only a matter of time for me though, so I decided to swim with larger fish and use as my defence, the fact that *my big brother is a fourth year.* Problem was, my shark wasn't to be seen in these waters. Nobody, including his teachers had ever seen my big brother at school this term. This was odd as I was walking to school with him in the mornings, but I had yet to spot him at any of the break times or wandering around in any of the school's buildings.
A month in and he even stopped walking into the school yard, choosing to blatantly bunk off and go and do his own thing. There goes my protection – not that I held any hope that big brother would rush to my aid.
In the end, I ended up not needing a protector as reputation was all I needed.

Contrary to urban legend, I was not a psycho. But then, what would you call a first year pupil who had a fight with a fourth year fat kid, got beaten good and proper, but still stood up and went back into the melee for more? Yep, some would call it madness.....but I called it a fluke. A fluke that was best I kept to myself.
I recognised him straight away. He was a fourth year. He was big in a flabby podgy way. Not big as in Johnny Weissmuller. He had fat hands and a fat neck and a Cypriot National Guard haircut. It was the barber's son and he recognised me too.
It was lunch break and I was chatting to some friends in a corner of the playground when the chubster came up to me and reminded me that I cried like a baby in his dad's shop. I of course took immediate offence and called him and his dad a couple of fat Pushtis (think I've explained the Greek meaning in an earlier chapter).
Maybe I overreacted, or felt I had to put on a front as my friends were watching, or perhaps I felt confident that the barber's son would not dare to start anything as my dad could beat up his dad (nothing childish about that). Whatever it was, it did put chubby in a difficult position...
He reluctantly punched me on the arm to show face in front of his friend I guess.

Can I just quickly explain that, even at that age, I knew my dad had a reputation amongst the Greek Cypriot community as a well-connected man. I'm not talking "Goodfellows" here or some mafioso with links to a criminal organisation. He survived as a restaurateur in the seventies in a rough part of

North London. He was beginning to be successful and make money. Some of his patrons did themselves have reputations and some even called on my dad as a friend.
This standing in the community was respected and was spoken about. I myself caught certain actions and was witness to some events in the restaurant that caused me to think of the old man differently. But this book is about me, so I won't dwell too much about suspicions and rumours regarding dad.
I could be wrong –I was young, so it is feasible I misconstrued things. Perhaps, after I complete this book, I'll write a prequel, not too dissimilar to The Godfather Part II, a look back at the younger dad and the rest of his villagers.
I'll may call it, An Awkward Immigrant - *The Cyprus Years!*

There was no force in the punch. For a fat kid, there was a fraction of the weight and power behind it. There was no doubt that he held back and perhaps was thinking of the consequences of beating up the son of one of his dad's respected customers. Of course it was too late.
<FIGHT!>
No sooner had that soft punch landed – and even that managed to floor me, the shout of *<FIGHT>* reverberated around the playground and no sooner had I got up, we were surrounded by a hundred-odd kids baying for blood.
I steamed back into him, arms flaying. There was no way I could get that fat neck into my famous head-lock, so I was relying on punches that only ever landed on a primary school age girl and that was only a half punch – which I still regret.

This time a two handed push floored me and again I got up but ran into a fist on the end of an arm held out in defence.
What I lacked in any fighting technique, I made up in pain tolerance. After all, I've been EPSd (ear-pop slapped) by the best of them.
Yep, I could have been mauled that day, but he refrained from doing me any real harm, even though I was a few years younger (which is a big deal in secondary school) and many stones lighter. I though, kept running back, punching and kicking and even tried a Chinese burn on one of those fat wrists.
As fights go, the crowd were not too displeased with the spectacle. It wasn't a classic, but to my advantage, some said that they saw a large kid pound on a smaller kid who never gave up. Others said that the smaller kid gave as good as he got, whilst others stated that had it not been for the teachers breaking up the fight, the plump kid would have been battered. One kid happened to mention to the others that Pan fought like a madman.
<Pan is a crazy.>
<Don't mess with Pan....he's a psycho.>
And so a "flukish" reputation was created.

In the days, weeks and months to come, I happened to notice that I wasn't picked on like others were – seems I wasn't worth the bother.
My reputation preceded me. So now I had to keep the status going, however, the problem was that I wasn't a good fighter. Getting into scrapes I would end up losing, would not only be

painful, but would eventually highlight to others that there was nothing to fear. I had to find a way to give myself that mad-man persona without the hurt. I needed to commit to acts of idiocy which can compensate for violence...

....and so started my school career as chief vandal, architect of all pranks and class disruptions.
Yep – what an idiot!

* * *

My first act of vandalism.

I was sent out of class one day, no doubt for being unruly or chatting – which to some teachers is one and the same.
The classroom was in the old block – the old Victorian building, where it was said, the ghosts of a former headmaster and pupil haunted the place. The boy's demise was at the hands of the headmaster, who had thrashed the boy to death, then took his own life by hanging himself.
Some rooms in that building had the original oak panelling and in some hallways on the top floors, they were adorned with green ceramic tiles from floor to waist height, crowned with a narrower black tile.
I sat on a chair outside the classroom bored, so I fished out my penknife with retractable can opener (and other useful tools like magnifying glass, flat screwdriver head, and scissors).

I started to scrape the grout away between the wall tiles (don't ask me why) and noticed that the hundred year old grout was coming away effortlessly. I chipped away a small section with the can opener tool that allowed me to then place the knife blade under the tile and with one levered movement, the tile popped off the wall....intact! I placed the tile carefully on the floor beside my chair and proceeded to the next. With its neighbouring tile missing, the next came off in no time. That tile was placed again carefully on top of its brother.
I was sent out the class within ten minutes of the lesson start time. That gave me thirty minutes to complete my task and one thing I had in those days was patience and resolve- a good trait amongst my many emotionalities.

The pips sounded over the speaker system announcing the end of period. Three beeps in succession which gave the teacher and pupils approximately thirty seconds to conclude the lesson and prepare to move onto the next. On hearing the pips, I dusted myself down and quickly went back down the hall and sat on the chair. Doors along the hall swung open and kids stormed out, including the class I sat outside.
The teacher who dismissed me from the class came out and stood above me with arms crossed. He looked down at me and I looked up with a butter wouldn't melt expression.
<I hope you've found boredom to your satisfaction young man and perhaps you've learnt a lesson,> he said.
In what seemed like slow motion, he looks back up and along the hallway as it empties of children going in various directions. The teacher has that look when your eyebrows

come down and you squint slightly. He notices a difference which he just can't place in those seconds and then a realisation. A realisation which is compounded when he looks back down at the pile beside me.
In neat rows and columns are half of the hallway's Victorian green wall tiles. I did break a few by accident, but I managed to get rid of those in the cleaner's cupboard.
Some of my friends who had waited at the end of the hallway for me, followed the teachers gaze and they too realised what I had done. One more for the reputation.
I was fiercely grabbed up by the arm and dragged away with him to the Head of Year.
<*Don't wait for me after school lads,*> I shout out, <*I may be late.*>

I can't keep asking for forgiveness every time I recount an incident of my past. I've apologised in almost every chapter, so without sounding like a right toss-pot, take it that regret has been expressed!

And not wanting to repeat myself...again....I'm sorry for some of the following short school stories........

* * *

Bugsy Malone...

The movie Bugsy Malone was released in 1976. The film was based on 1920s American gangsters during prohibition. It would have been a good film had it not been for the cast which

was entirely made up of children playing gangsters, dancers and gangsters' moles dressed provocatively. A Jimmy Saville wank-a-thon.
I didn't see the film when it came out in the cinema, but I hated it then as I hate it now. Let's just say that it is not my cup-of-tea.
Being asked to act out various scenes in drama class could have been a nightmare, but in my school nightmares were turned to our advantage.
I don't think I'll be apologising for this school tale...........

That year we had a new drama teacher. A failed classical actor with the obligatory brown corduroys and a matching corduroy satchel. He wore Jesus-creepers on his feet and he had a cord on his glasses which he used as a dramatic prop. He was hell bent on making our one and only easy-time lesson hard work. He arrived to work with the script of Bugsy Malone and announced to us that by the end of this term, we (our class) would perform selected scenes of Bugsy to the whole school. This will be his directorial debut which will lead to a new career outside of this all boys madhouse of a school. Or so he thought.

He split us into four groups of approximately seven to each group and gave us a script and a dedicated corner of the drama class to read, learn lines and rehearse our scene.
Throughout the lesson and the following weeks, he would visit each group, remonstrate, have a bitch-fit and walk off in a huff. We in turn would sit back down in our groups and continue our discussions and perusal of topless women

pictures. Those with older brothers who were lent pictures of Chesty Morgan to bring into school were treated as the popular kids.

I think I have mentioned Chesty Morgan in a previous chapter or two. For the few of you who don't know, Chesty had a seventy-three inch bust and was the star of classic B-movies called "Deadly Weapons" (you can guess what those weapons were...the clue is in the "double") and "Double Agent 73" (73 is a clever reference to the size of Chesty's breasts).
I had not seen those movies then, but relied on my older brother and his friends to give me a full appraisal and on one very special occasion, a cut-out picture of Chesty Morgan's assets.
Yes, sadly I have recently Youtubed Chesty and wish I hadn't as the whole mystic surrounding Chesty has now gone.

A few weeks had past – around six to eight drama lessons worth and the drama teacher was fretting and ruining our quality time. He went from group to group shouting at the lack of any real improvement of acting or the fact that lines to scenes had not been learnt at all! He threatened us with detention and regardless of what we had achieved (which wasn't much), he would force us to perform whatever we had learnt to the whole school.
This was unacceptable to us and we agreed amongst ourselves that we had to do something about it.

There was a tried and tested method that was discovered by accident which always worked to discourage any drama teacher's illusions of grandeur. It was called – The Bundle.

We got our act together (pun). We half learnt our scenes and we agreed that each group would rehearse to the teacher and to the other groups in the middle of the drama room for critique and input.

My group was first up. We took our positions in the middle of the room and cleared our throats. The teacher was rubbing his thighs with excitement.

I can't remember the movie scene itself but I know I was playing Fat Sam and I was shouting at one of my men.

There were further lines spoken by other characters and it was all quite dramatic............and then we went off scene and straight to a random fight scene.

The seven of us got into a theatrical fight which resulted in a pile of us in the middle of the room screaming, shouting, headlocking and slapping.

And then the bundle followed to the shouts of *<NO>* from the teacher and *<BUNDLEEEE>* from the class.

All the other kids rushed and bundled – piled onto their peers. The mound of boys was getting higher to real screams of the unfortunate ones trapped on the bottom tiers. Some kids with old scores to settle took this opportunity to stick the boot into the backs of kids trapped, and who would have no idea who kicked them as their heads were entombed under someone's fat arse.

This was the classic Bundle.

It took the drama teacher ten whole minutes to disengage the bundle and separate the four groups into their respective corners.
As punishment and a warning for the others, my group was informed that we would be on detention that evening and possibly on report if we repeated such an incident.
After a brief period of reflection and on gaining class order, the teacher instructed the next group to the middle to perform their scene.
The next scene starred characters Bugsy, Knuckles and some gangsters. Knuckles ended up being floored with the gangsters on top and then the shout of *<BUNDLE>* rang across the room. Once again, the whole class dived on top of one another and this one only slightly more violent than the last.
My group were marked for detention so with nothing to lose except a kidney, we too bundled.

You would have thought the teacher would have got the message by then, but no, he had to experience all four scenes of mayhem, fights and screams. By Bundle number four, there was heavy retaliation by those who were kicked in previous scenes.
In the end, we achieved what we set out to do and that was the last we heard of Bugsy Malone.

I walked home with a bloody nose that day. Others with bad backs, sprained ankles and black eyes.

It was a hefty price to pay but let's be honest - think of the poor sod who was to play Tallulah in front of the whole school of boys!

* * *

My broken tooth. A British Bulldog tale.

One more thing to add to my perceived disadvantages!
I count myself fortunate and blessed to be born without any physical disabilities, but it didn't stop me back then from unashamedly asking <*Why me God? Haven't you heaped enough on me?*>

At thirteen and a half years of age, I broke my front tooth – in half! They weren't the straightest or cleanest of teeth, but a goofy smile is better than no smile.
If there were injury lawyers back then I would have sued my school. I mean what kind of idiot introduces British Bulldog to a P.E lesson at an all-boys school in Holloway?

The game (if you can call it a game) British Bulldog pits one man (or boy) against the horde. The rules are such – there are no rules. The object of the game is to evade capture by any means possible. The Bulldog – the poor sod chosen at random, stands in the middle of the play area. In my case it was the

school gym surrounded by concrete walls and a solid concrete floor. The rest of the players (which could total any number, but that day there were thirty of them) stand at one end of the wall. On the blow of the P.E teacher's whistle, the horde run like flipping lunatics to the opposite end of the gym, avoiding being captured by the idiot stood there in the middle with his arms held wide in hope that a fellow idiot runs into his arms.
If by a small miracle the Bulldog is able to capture and hold one of the opposition for more than three seconds, the captured idiot joins forces with the Bulldog. On another blow of the whistle, the remaining twenty nine run back in the direction they started from, but this time they have to avoid the two sad bastards in the middle.
The supposed winner of the game is the one captured at the end. However, by that time, several fights would have broken out and it was very unlikely that the game would last till the end.

One day, I was chosen to be the Bulldog. Not by random though. I was chosen because I was speaking when the P.E teacher was. I was probably saying what nice trainers the teacher had on and could he see them with his fat belly sticking out!
I'll say this now. I hated P.E teachers the most.
In my school, the ones that only taught P.E were overweight fat-arses who took pride in embarrassing kids who were poor at sports – Football in particular! Small Asian kids in particular and in addition to the previous in particular ...followed by the Greek kids...in that order!

They would have outwardly hated the black kids too, but most were good at sports.
I'm touching on dodgy ground here, but truth be told....1970s London was rife with racism – more so in sports.
Anyway, let's not darken the mood. The chapter subtitle gives away the ending, so you've guessed by now that I am bitter with the outcome.
To my old P.E teachers out there, sitting in their incontinence pants.....go ahead and sue me!

I'm stood in the middle of the arena. I feel like Victor Mature in the classic film Demetrius and the Gladiators.
I wasn't the biggest of kids, but I wasn't the smallest either. My tactic was to aim for the smallest kid first. Then build up an army of small kids who would then be able to pick off a medium size kid...and so on.
Nature has many examples where smaller animals work as one to bring down the larger animal. It is called pack-hunting.
But first, you need a pack!

The whistle blew. Thirty boys of all sizes roared and then bombed it full speed towards me. The loud shriek of the whistle and the thunderous sound of thirty kids caused me to hesitate. I lost sight of one small kid I had my eye on. Before I could track him down, all thirty of them made it to the opposite wall. When they reached the wall, they turned around and taunted me. Some with two-finger salutes and the more mature boys amongst them gave me the five-knuckle-shuffle sign.
I moved back to the middle and readied myself again.

I tracked down a different smaller kid this time. A short chubby one. Less nimble.
Once again, the whistle blew and once again, this was followed by battle screams. The larger kids ran past me unfazed. A few smaller athletic kids, dodged and swerved in and out of my way. I ignored them and kept my eye on my intended target. He saw that I had marked him for take-down.
With all but my intended prey now at the opposite wall, I moved forward with hands ready to grasp. Then the shit puts his head down and makes a charge. He hit me in the gut. He sent me flying on my arse. He made it to the wall.
This was embarrassing. I quickly dusted myself down and turned for the next stampede. This time my target was a medium sized skinny kid.

The whistle went again. This time I ran first. I headed straight for the skinny kid and I was the one screaming.
The skinny kid backed away. He headed back to the starting wall. I ran at full pelt. His back was against the wall. There was no escape. I was like a juggernaut and I was gonna flatten him. This was Death Race 2000 (the 1975 film not the crappy remake)! He sidestepped. I couldn't stop in time. I went head first into the wall at forty miles an hour (give or take thirty five miles). I felt my forehead smack the wall first, then my nose, followed quickly by my mouth. One second later I was lying on my back, arms spread out.
I saw stars and I heard angels crying.
Fifteen seconds later, the P.E teacher was looking down at me (unconcerned) and behind him were the thirty kids.

I shook and cleared my head. I realised it wasn't angels but kids laughing. There was a throb coming from my mouth. I sat up. I must not show weakness. I touched my mouth with my fingers and inspected them. There was blood.
<*Blood!*> I cried out.
I went to put my tongue on my lips and as it brushed by my front teeth, I felt a stabbing pain which started from my tooth and ended up running down my spine and looped back into my balls! I touched my mouth, then my teeth and then a sharp tooth.
<*BLOOOOOODDDDDD!*> I screamed to a roar of laughter from thirty kids and a P.E teacher dressed in a Jimmy Saville track suit.

* * *

Another fight – hold me back.

As the secondary school years ticked by, it was getting harder to avoid fights by a reputation of some sort of pseudo-idiot. There was a fight looming but I wasn't worried. I was no stranger to fighting, but I hadn't had one in ages. Not only that, I had yet to beef out like some of the other kids in my year. But not to worry, I had speed and I could take punishment and pain.....or so I thought.
This kid was asking for it. He was a couple of inches shorter than me, but he had developed those post puberty wide shoulders and his back was a V-shape. His arms looked bigger

too, or it could be his tight blazer giving that effect. Regardless, he was acting hard and I had enough of his jibes.
<*Oi, after class alwight.*> I said in my macho cockney accent.
He decided he couldn't wait after class. He squared up to me and said <*Yeah?*>
And I said <*Yeah,*> back
<*Yeah?*> he says again
<*Yeah.*> I said and pushed him back.
He must have took offence to my push. I didn't see them coming. He threw a fast-as-lightening combination of punches aimed at my head. One, two and then three. All fast, all hard and all three punches making contact.
Where the heck did that come from? My head was throbbing. My eye was closing. I stormed in blindly. I tried to storm in (you know, rush in, punches swinging), but he side-stepped and threw two more punches...again to my head.
This kid never heard of body shots or headlocks?
I used my psycho roar to try and scare him, but that spurned him to throw yet another combination.
I was in trouble, no doubt about that.
Lucky for me, this took place during class and the teacher (a nice female teacher who I thought had the hots for me) instructed some of our classmates to break us up. So two large kids grabbed my arms and pulled me back and another two pushed my opponent back, which he calmly obliged.

This was a disaster as well as painful.
Yeah, I've been hit before (mainly by mum) but this was Bad – with a capital B!

I've never felt my face swell up in real time before. I counted my heartbeats by touching my reddening cheekbone.
I had to save face. I had to show everybody that I was not in any pain or affected in any way.
I started struggling against the two kids holding me. A third kid joined them as I was thrashing in their arms......
<*Hold me back, or I'll kill im'*.> I screamed
<*Hold me back!*>
<*I'm gonna fucking kill im', hold me backkkkk.*>
Thank fuck they held me back.....but then I had to push it.
<*Let me go and his a dead ma..........oh Bollocks*>
I didn't even have time to finish the words "dead man". Those bastards went and let me go.
This time he threw some body punches (spoke to soon I guess) and I swear I felt my breast plate snap and heard my right kidney pack its bags to visit his brother kidney over on the left side of my body. I was bent over.
To my surprise and everlasting gratitude, this kid held his ground and ceased in my torture. He knew he had won and luckily for me, he wasn't an idiot such as I was.
That day taught me a valuable lesson – always pick fights you can win.

We became mates after that day.
He told me that he had taken up boxing because there weren't many black kids like him living on the mainly white housing estate. I told him that he should have told me that much earlier.

Ten years after that fight, I heard through the Holloway grapevine that he died of Leukaemia.

* * *

Quink

Quink or Quick-Ink was sold in bottles and developed by the Parker Pen Company for use in Parker and other fountain pens. Due to declines in handwriting standards, we were encouraged to bring into school fountain pens (and ink). This proved not to be the best idea my school had. Most days we would go home covered in the blue stuff, but it was only when one of the teachers ended up with an old pensioner's blue rinse that the school decided to ban fountain pens in favour of Biros.

It was during a chemistry class. The chemistry teacher insisted on silence during an impromptu chemistry test. Needless to say, some of us were pretty pissed off as we hadn't revised – not that any revision would have helped, since not one of us had any interest in chemistry and had shown this by our disruptive behaviour.
The chemistry teacher wore a clean white lab coat. I suppose this emphasised his intelligence to the other teachers in the staff room. It showed up the P.E teachers who arrived to work in tight tracksuits which showed off their fat arses and the six-pack of beers they drank during the weekend.
The art teachers were unfazed by a lab coat dressed in their cool purple corduroy trousers, as were the drama teachers in their brown corduroys.

Don't ask me why, but the scruffiest lot in my school were the history & geography teachers. One department for both subjects and a baggy suit between the lot!
Now you will think that I am stereotyping or making this up, but the two female French teachers wore short skirts and tight tops, which drove those of us approaching the hard-on years crazy. The hard-on years, for those who did not go through puberty at an all-boys school was a time when we unashamedly walked around with stiffies in our pants... (especially after a French lesson) to proudly display, like male ballet dancers, our groin protuberances - announcing that we are men......and fuck were we stupid to come to an all-boys school in the first place!

As if to emphasise that I am writing this on the hoof, I just remembered a history teacher we had, who in one double lesson explained in great detail, how back in his homeland of Zaire (now called the Democratic Republic of the Congo) he rescued his sister from vampires and then proceeded to cleanse his village of the bloodsuckers.
He described in graphic detail how he stalked, then captured and then drove wooden stakes into vampires' hearts. For eighty minutes (a double lesson) there was not one peep out of the thirty strong class of boys.
Until today, I'd forgotten all about that day. Thanks book!

Where was I?
The chemistry teacher walked up and down the classroom between the desk aisles. He wore his unsoiled white lab coat to

show us plebs that he indeed was a scientist and that we were nothing...
But to us - he was a target!
(*See what I mean about sociably awkward*).
As he walked past me, I turned from my desk to look behind. I raised my Parker fountain pen after sucking up as much Quink the pen's reservoir could hold and with a flick-of-a-wrist on the end of an arm swipe, my Parker pen released an ink jet of blue ink that splattered the clean white lab coat, leaving a blue Rorschach blot which one could describe as two moths or butterflies facing back to back. I saw two human shapes in that blue pattern and one was holding a rolling pin.
Those looking up at that time gasped and then exhaled when there was no reaction from the teacher. Those looking down, looked up and wondered why those had gasped and then gasped themselves twenty-three seconds later when the chemistry teacher reached the end wall, about-turned and came back down the aisle.

In the time it took me to unscrew the pen's plastic body, dip the nib in the bottle of Quink, squeeze the pen's reservoir rubber bladder, suck up the ink, re-screw the cap, the teacher had reached my desk. I managed to get in two quick swipes of the arm and wrist just as he passed my desk.
Another direct hit, but this time not a blob but two blue streaks, from left shoulder blade to right shoulder blade then slanting to left buttock.
I had created two of the three lines in the Mark of Zorro.
For those who do not know Zorro....

Zorro - He makes the sign of the Z, (pronounced zee)
Zorro - The fox of cunning and creed...
Zorro.........

A hold of breath........then an exhalation of breath.
Again, he didn't feel it.
<He must have starched the shit out of that lab coat.>
Street Legend status goes up a notch. Psycho Pan's at it again.
The whole class is enthralled. Faces light up and I have a shit-eating grin.
The game is afoot. I have to complete the sign of the Zee.
The good news is that it was a new bottle of Quink.
The walk down towards the front of the class takes slightly longer. As always, I am sat at the back. This gives me more time to calmly reload and position myself in my seat for a better angle to achieve a streak and not a blob on his return to the back of the class. As before, facing the back when the desk faces the front is going to be a problem achieving a blue streak, but if anybody is capable, that kid is me!

(Just a reminder that I am not proud of what I did, but I have to get into young Pan-mode to get the story accurately across).
I'm locked and loaded. He strides past. The whole class is watching his back. I'm too excited and all of a sudden, I'm dying for a piss. I hesitate. He is two feet further than last time.
A nudge in my back and I let loose with a sideways sweep. I miss and hit a kid on the opposite bank of desks.
The teacher has his back to me, time is of the essence. I could sit back down and wait for the return run, but I'm too

impatient. I stand up and like a lion tamer whipping at a lion who's just about to lunge and take the tamer's balls in his jaws, I strike away like a madman. I'm swishing and swiping and lunging with my fountain pen.
Ink is going in all directions, from collar to arse, from hip to spine. Blue ink is raining down on the once white lab coat. There is uproar of laughter from the whole class.
The teacher turns on his heels and blue ink streaks his face and neck and paints his eyebrows blue and actually gives him blue handle bar eyebrows. Like Mustapha's bushy eyebrows.....but blue!

Mustapha was the first in our year to get pubic hair as well as a hairy back and chest.
When we'd go swimming with the school at the rat-infested Caledonian Road Swimming Pool (by the way, it's a posh leisure centre now), Mustapha would walk around the changing rooms with no towel around his waist!

Some ink goes inside the chemistry teacher's mouth when he's just about to shout out. A blob splats on his top lip giving him an ominous Adolf look – *<Jawohl, mein Führer.>*

I am out of ink. I am out of luck. But I am in for it!
I failed to complete the sign of the Zee.

My parents were sent a cleaning bill and funnily enough, I had the sign of the Zee slapped across my arse. Still, I was coming to the end of being beaten and slapped about at home, so not much of a deterrent there.

* * *

The final years of school.

I'm happy to say that not all the school years were wasted.
I was maturing. I was looking forward to a future outside school. Home life was not getting any easier, just moving into other situations which I had to adapt to. The pranks were becoming less frequent. Yes, there were some minor mindless escapades, but nothing to write a whole sub-chapter on.
I lit some Bunsen burners in science and left them on during break. Came back to a really warm classroom. Filled up some balloons with sand and water and chucked them into the science block's extractor fans – which made a hell of a grinding noise. Oh, shit, nearly forgot. I tore the thick curtains in the cinema room. When I say tore, I mean I shredded them. It started off as an accident. I was sitting next to the window and I noticed one of the curtains frayed at the bottom. So I grabbed both ends at the bottom and when I pulled at the tear, the curtain made a ripping sound as it split from bottom all the way to the top. They egged me on, so I did them all.
By the time the teacher walked in, the curtains resembled doorway beads.

We pelted the ice-cream van man with snowballs... ......actually that was funny.

He was a Greek guy and he was funny too. Such a nice man. He would park outside the school at lunchtimes and would sell hotdogs and hamburgers as well as crisps and ice-lollies.
My favourite was the banana lolly.
<A banana lolly for my banana friend,> he would always say when I would buy one.
He was under strict orders from the head that he must not sell anything outside lunch hours, so he would sit in his van and at dead-on 12 o'clock, he would slide the glass window of his van, lean out and greet the waiting hoard with *<Hello my lovely boys.>*
One winter's day, with the ground covered in snow, the ice-cream man counted down the minutes and seconds to 12 o'clock. We all stood waiting with arms behind our backs.
Dead on twelve, he gets up from the driver's chair and goes to the side window. With a cheerful expression, he slides the window wide open, leans out and greets us with *<Hello my lovely……>*
He didn't have time to finish his sentence. Twenty-five snowballs pelted him and the inside of his van simultaneously. Then two seconds later, another twenty-five snowballs were launched towards his van.
The second twenty-five volley gave time for the first team to reload and salvo another round.

If you've seen the film Zulu (with Michael Caine and Stanley Baker) then you will know that the next few sentences are pure fiction, but to me at that time, the bombardment of the van with snowballs was like a scene from Zulu.

I am almost sure I heard someone shout.....
<Volley by ranks!
First rank, FIRE!
Second rank, FIRE!
Third rank, FIRE!>
<Followed by – fire at will.>
The ice-cream man, I would like to think, screamed out <*Zulus to the south west. Thousands of them.*>
The van was being rocked by the endless volley of snowballs. The guy struggled to close the window and took some direct hits to the head and body. Eventually he managed to close up, get in the driver's seat and drive away to the last of the aerial rounds hitting the roof of the van.

Man it was cold that day. As we all looked around in some sort of sick triumph, some smart arse reminded us that it was too late to queue up for school dinners!

I should have written that as a sub-chapter. Never mind.
Actually, I'm struggling to remember anything worthwhile of mentioning. So time to move off the secondary school chapter, but if I come up with anything else – normally it's in the middle of the night– I'll add it to the miscellaneous chapter at the end of the book. Or I could cheat and insert a chapter 12A.

I was reaching an age where the prospect of leaving school was playing on my mind. I didn't know which direction my life would go in, but there was one thing I was certain of. I didn't want to work in my dad's restaurant.

I had started the fourth year, the beginning of the two year O-level studies. It was time to knuckle down and get something from the last two years.

I would like to say I was mature enough to consider options and pull my school life around, but that would be bullshit. My school turnaround was down to two things.

1. Mr Powell. Head of English and form tutor. Immediately after the latest stupid act of vandalism, Mr Powell takes me to the Head's office but instead of an instant punishment, or boring lecture, he just sits in a chair opposite me and starts to read some paperwork. Then he starts marking worksheets and humming to himself. He ignores me totally, like I am not even there. An hour later he dismisses me without a word being said during that hour. Or if he did say anything, I can't remember it. I only remember the way I was ignored, like I was nothing. I wanted a confrontation, but he never obliged.

I stand to leave and as I open the door, he looks up from his work and says to me *<Is this what your life will amount to Panico? Will you be happy wasting your time?>*

Somehow he got me thinking about the future.

2. My school introduces a new O-level subject. Electronics. You couldn't do electronics unless you chose physics – so I took both. In the first few weeks of studying these subjects I discovered that I was an electronic whizz. Not Stephen Hawking's whizz, but a Holloway Whizz.

I understood, diodes and transistors and resistors and basic circuitry. I learnt the resistor colour code and brought magazines so that I could build electronic gadgets like a two-stage amplifier or a simple radio receiver to work in conjunction with the two stage amp.
My new found appreciation to learn turned me from the secondary school year-one-through-to-year-three idiot, into a year four-to-year-five geek. I got the second highest test score in physics and the highest in electronics. Shit, I was even starting to think about staying on at sixth form – which only one-in-twenty pupils did.
The sixth formers had their own chill-out room where they could play poker and could even smoke. Yep, sixth form was becoming a real option for me.

My dad attended the last parents' evening before the final exams. Actually, it was the first time any of my parents attended a parents' evening or in fact, any meeting that the school had requested my parents attend during my erratic years.
I introduced dad to Mr Powell who was more than happy to discuss my surprising academic turnaround and predicted exam results and perhaps even moving onto A-levels.
My dad tells Mr Powell that it was no surprise to him because I was always the smartest one and that my future is in the restaurant business and not working for wages in some dead-end company – like Rumbelows!
As my dad stands up ready to leave the meeting (dad decided there and then there was nothing further to discuss), he

pauses, then pulls out his wallet and fishes out his restaurant business card. He hands it over and says that Mr Powell and his family are welcome anytime (preferably on a weekday though) to come and eat at a discount.

As it turned out, all the electronic companies that I wrote to seeking apprenticeship like Thorn, Marconi, Radio Rentals and so on, all ceased operating, so maybe I should have gone into serving Meze and T-bone steaks at the Taverna. But I wasn't to know that then.
Regardless, I had to decide my future. It was my decision to make, not dad's.
I would decide my next steps after the O-level results. In the meantime, I promised dad that I would work full time in the restaurant over the summer – a sort of "suck-it-and-see" trial.

End of the day – I survived secondary school where others failed.
Actually, that sounds stupid. It wasn't borstal I attended!!
I'm just getting into the head of a melodramatic teen who is about to leave school and his emotions are getting the better of him. After I complete this book, I will most likely have to see a shrink in order to purge the young Pan out of me!
I think what I meant to say at the start of this paragraph was that after all the shit I pulled off, I ended up with some sort of education and qualifications that got me by in my chosen career. I am aware that some (not all) of my classmates ended up in dead-end menial employment and a few even ended up

in prison - but not all. Some of my buddies fared much better and went away to university. Anyway, in the end, I think I was sad to leave school. It's a big step.
The next years saw me in good employment, but I was far from happy in my home life. What is a working life if your home life amounts to nothing?

Time to move on. I'll come back to home life post school years later. There is a *post scriptum* – an addendum, which I would like include which will conclude my school years......

CHAPTER 12A:-HOLLOWAY WOMEN'S PRISON.

I have decided to put this tale in its own chapter rather than a sub-chapter as it takes place off school grounds and a mile away from the safety of my neighbourhood.

Holloway Prison is up for sale now with no sitting tenants. They moved the ladies out and shut up shop. Islington Council plan to have the site redeveloped into affordable luxury apartments for those who can afford the indulgence of mortgaging to the hilt. Sadly, it won't be fellow Hollowaynians buying these homes.

The prison was just over a stone's throw away from our school. One day a rumour spread throughout the whole school that excited most of the younger boys – including myself.
The rumour was about a kid who lived in a block of flats in an estate at the rear of the prison. He was riding his bike along a path which ran parallel to the rear prison blocks. As he rode slowly by, he heard a lady's harsh voice call out *<ere darling, come an ave a butchers at these.>*
Apparently all incarcerated women in Holloway talk like Eliza Doolittle.

For those who are not wise to the way of The Cockneys, the term "have a butchers" is Cockney rhyming slang for having a look. Butcher's Hook – Look!
Londoners also use the phrase – "have a Gander at this". But "avin a Gander" is not Cockney. It comes from humble rural folk-talk adopted by Londoners. To Goosey Gander – in other words -stretch one's neck to have a look. Just like geese do.
The great thing about Cockney rhyming slang is that it is always evolving with time.
Nowadays nobody knows what a Butcher's Hook is because we all buy our meat ready prepared in meals. No longer can you see animal carcases hanging off hooks in the butcher's shop window. Those more adventurous, buy meat in plastic trays with a picture of a cow or sheep stuck on the front. That way, you are made aware that lamb comes from sheep and beef comes from horses. Chicken comes from chicken!
So today's modern Cockneys might say something like – "Have a Kelly". I.e. Kelly Brooke – look.
Kelly Brooke – is a famous actress. She starred in the 2010 movie Piranha 3D. A remake of the classic 1978 Piranha.

Anyway, let us get back to my Captain Cook, as I am just about to mention some Georgie Bests!

When the lad in question looks up towards the rear prison cell blocks, he notices hands waving through the iron bars fixed outside the windows. Then hands disappear and reappear holding ladies bras. (I wouldn't know the difference between men's and women's bras myself).

The kid gets off his bike and walks nearer to the perimeter wall and this time when he takes another look up towards the top level windows, he sees a couple of ladies pressed up against the bars...topless!
<*Wat yer fink of these mister?*> they shout out whilst shaking their breasts side to side, then up and down.
The boy, now with his first ever glimpse of boobs burnt into his retinas, runs off thrilled with images that will see him through a few nights of sock-hand action.
Then he returns and picks up his bike.

The story reached my ears whilst gambling with my mates in the gambling pitch.
<*I knew it!*> I exclaimed to the messenger. <*My older brother told me one of his mates saw the same thing a few years back.*>
Obviously, the lady must have committed a heinous crime to still be at it in jail!
<*When are we going?*> One of my friends asks.
<*Let's go tomorrow, then I can bring the binoculars I got free with Whizzer and Chips!*>
Whizzer and Chips was the working boys' comic to the posh kids The Dandy.
<*Hang on,*> I add. <*We have to go through "The Estate" to get to the rear prison wall.*>

If this book gets made into a movie, I would like the sound editor to add the dramatic sound effect -Dun Dun Duuuun, when the young actor playing me says <*We have to go through "The Estate."*>

Or a horse cry, like in the film Young Frankenstein, whenever they mentioned the name Frau Blücher.
<*We have to go through "The Estate."*> Neighhhhhhhhh-brrrr.

Only kids who live on The Estate behind the prison are allowed on The Estate. Postmen don't go to The Estate, only Coppers, and in pairs, armed in riot gear and tear gas!
Me and some friends once made the mistake of venturing on Estate Turf! We didn't know the rules. We were looking for a shortcut home from school, when we came across a play area with swings and slides. No sooner than my arse sat on a swing, five Skinheads came out from wherever they were staking-out from and chased us away with broken bottles and homemade Nunchunks (Nunchunks may be covered in a later chapter if I get time). We had a narrow escape and never set foot in that area again.

<*Oh shit I forgot,*> another one of my mate says.
<*But if a whole load of us go, it won't be a problem,*> I finish to a chorus of nods.
<*So spread the news. Tomorrow after school, a large group of us will go through "The Estate"* (Dun Dun Duuuun, Neighhhhhh-brr) *and check out the topless ladies.*>

The next day I arrived at school with my free plastic binoculars. The plan was to skip the last lesson, go and get a Chip-Butty, then make our way to the prison.
During break-time we tried to track down the kid who had seen the prisoners flashing their wares. I went up to the kid

who brought me the news and he said that he heard the story from another kid. By the end of first break, we tracked down the kid who heard it off the kid who heard it from another kid. We were getting close to the source. By lunch-time break, we failed to track down the original kid, but another kid swore blindly that he too saw prisoners shaking their stuff. This particular kid was not credible, especially since he wore milk-bottle-bottom glasses. At last break, we gave up on finding the kid. We assumed he must still be at home with his sock.
We arranged to meet at the bakers in Brecknock Road and went back to the final lesson of the day.

Later that day, thirty school boys arrived at the bakery. Only twenty had money to buy a Chip-Butty, which was good because you needed an even number.

Interlude – The Chip-Butty.

The Holloway Chip-Butty is legendary. I don't know who started it, but whoever did must be kicking himself for not getting a patent to protect his Butty invention as he has missed out on thousands of pounds in royalties.
The reason you needed an even number for it to work is as follows...
You buy a loaf of fresh bread – not sliced, and you ask the lady in the bakery to cut it in half. Across the middle of the loaf, not downwards! Then you hand the half loaf of bread to your mate and you both proceed to the chippy in Torriano Avenue. Whilst walking to the chippy, you would scoop out the bread and

throw it on the pavement. The idea is to hollow out the loaf of bread, leaving just the crust. By the time you reach the chip-shop, you should be holding a scooped-out half of a large loaf of bread.
You then enter the chip-shop and hand the half loaf to the greasy guy with the dirty apron behind the counter. He then fills up the hollowed-out loaf with five pounds (in weight) of chips – costing fifty pence.
It goes without saying that you will want tomato ketchup. The chip-shop guy doesn't even ask. He takes the filled up loaf to the watered down (with vinegar) ketchup dispenser and proceeds to pump out one pint of the stuff all over the chips. The ketchup is so watered down (with vinegar) that it sinks down to the bottom of the loaf, coating every single chip on its way. He then hands you the Chip-Butty and you have to grasp it with both hands whilst leaning slightly back so that the Butty does not topple you forward.
Before your mate gets his half, he has to open the door for you so that you can exit. He then has to ask the guy behind the counter to let him out.

End of interlude – back to the story.

Thirty boys left the bakery and headed for the chip-shop.
Thirty boys and one hundred pigeons following on route arrived at the chip-shop. A half hour later, twenty boys who could barely walk, accompanied by another ten boys who made do with the discarded arse of the Chip-Butties made their way to The Estate.

We all bought a can of Coke each and when we all drank the cans empty, we started to kick thirty empty cans of Coke towards our destination.
If you happen to kick the can into the road, you were not allowed to pick it up and you were out of the game. The only time a can is permitted to go into the road is when the kicker crosses said road. Once you cross the road, the skill is to get the cans over the kerbstone and back onto the footpath.
There was an element of anticipation in the air so we quickened our pace leaving the cans behind us.

Thirty young boys of all shapes, sizes and colours arrived onto The Estate, notorious for being a skinhead haunt and headed straight out again to the rear boundary wall of the prison.
We made it. Safety in numbers saw us enter and leave without a hitch.
<*That's the prison.*> A kid yelled whilst pointing to the prison!
<*YEAH.*> We all yelled in triumph.
We all followed the path around the rear of the site. Some were impatient and made it known. Some were arguing amongst themselves.
<*Where's the windows with the bars?*>
<*I'd be fucked if I know.*>
<*I thought you knew where it happened.*>
<*Why would I know?*>
<*Do you think we'll see some tits?*>
<*You are a tit – where's the windows with the bars?*>
<*Do I look like the fucking warden?*>
<*Let's keep going. Round that corner.*>

<*Who you calling a tit?*>
<*We can always go round your house and see your mum's tits.*>
<*Oi Frying-Pan. You got those binoculars?*>
<*Why? Can't you find your prick?*>
<*At least I have one.*>
<*At least I know what to do with one.*>
<*The path ends here and there's no windows with bars.*>
<*I bet that little shit was lying.*>
<*Do you know who he is then?*>
<*No, I thought you did.*>
<*You're the one who told me yesterday.*>
<*Mate, there's no windows with bars. All those small square windows look fucking one foot thick.*>
<*My knobs that thick.*>
<*Your mum's knob is that thick.*>
<*It's Frying-Pan's fault.*>
<*What?*>
Just then, our exchange is interrupted by a deep voice coming from behind us.
<*Excuse us lads, but can you stop there for a minute.*>
We all turn around and we all stop talking. Some of us are heard to gulp!
Approaching us are two policemen. One with a flat cap and stripes on his uniform and the other younger and much taller with a "Bobbies" helmet.
<*What are you boys doing here then?*> Flat-cap asks.
<*Nothing Sir,*> most of us say in unison.
<YOU!> Flat-cap raised his voice and points to one of my friends who just happened to be standing nearest to them.

<*What are you boys doing hanging around the back of the Her Majesty's Prison?*>

<*We were going to the play area and got lost.*>

<*Nice one.*> I whispered.

Then the younger policeman steps nearer and says, <*you lads aint here to see the ladies showing off there titties are you?*>

Flat-cap has a chuckle as the younger one continues. <*As you can see, the windows were replaced some years back with glass blocks, so if you came here hoping to see topless ladies, then you boys have had a wasted journey.*>

<*What school are you boys from?*> Flat-cap asks.

<*The all-boys school in Holloway,*> a few of us replied.

<*Thought so,*> the younger policeman says with a smirk.

<*You've had your legs pulled. We get you kids here every few years. Be on your way now and don't come back. We will be informing your school by the way.*>

With heads dropped, we all walk passed the policemen and make our way silently through The Estate.

Once out of earshot, our thirty-way conversation starts up again.

<*Yes sir Mr. Policeman.*> someone mimics.

<*Didn't here you say shit.*>

<*That's because he was shitting himself.*>

<*Is that why you got a damp patch on your crotch?*>

<*Wait till I find that git who said he saw tits.*>

<*Hey lads...*>

<*He probably saw your tits in P.E.*>

<*Perv...*>

<*Poofter.*>

<Hey lads....>
<Old chubby here has bigger tits then your mum.>
<Your mum's back at that prison, maybe it was her waving her tits!>
<LADS.>
<Well there's no chance of seeing his mum's tits then. Let's go to your house!>
<His mum's got no tits.>
<Yes she has....I mean no she hasn't ...I mean...oh fuck off.>
<Hahaha, make your mind up. Does she have tits or not?>
<HEY LADS!>
<WHAT?>
<SKINHEADS, COMING OUT OF THE ESTATE.>
DUN DUN DUUUUN..........
NEIGHHHHHHH-BRR

* * *

CHAPTER 13:-RESTAURANTS (OLD AND NEW) AND INTRODUCING - ALEXIA

From an early age I had always helped in my dad's restaurants. He had two restaurants. The old one spanned the Mayton Street years and the new one was opened and kept going during the Pakeman Street years.
When the Pakeman Street years ended for me, my dad's marriage and business ended for him.
He divorced, sold up and went back to Cyprus.
I never found the right time in later years to ask him why. Time just simply ran out. We reacquainted, then he passed away.
I wanted to ask why leave his wife and kids then and not five or ten years prior? Why not five years later?
I'd like to think that he was ready for retirement and that's why he sold his life's work. But in the back of my mind, I think that he thought by leaving, he was doing it for all our sakes.

The restaurant(s) were all our lives' work. My father's, my mother's and all of us kids.

* * *

The Old Restaurant

-started off as a late night Steak House.
The clientele was a bit on the rough side and most weeks there would be trouble of one kind or another. My father had to keep an Irish Shalalie behind the bar to restore order from time to time. The Shalalie was a gift from a big Irishman who swore to the Shalalie's peace-keeping properties. It also passed as wall decoration which would confirm the police statement that no weapons were found on-site when they would haul off either a bloodied dazed drunk patron for refusing to pay his bill, or unconscious dickheads who just wanted to start trouble.
As kids, we knew when my dad had trouble at the restaurant because we would see the blood stains on the table cloths my mum took to the launderette. Sometimes, mum would have to put them in the washing machine twice over to get rid of the stains. Other times, she would cut them and sew them into tea-towels if it was a rougher night than usual.
Eventually, dad had to lower the closing hours to avoid the late night drunks. He started to open earlier and changed the menu.

He introduced Greek food to the menu. This attracted the local poker-playing patrons from the Greek Coffee House next door. A group of hard-core gamblers became regulars and they enjoyed the selection of Greek dishes accompanied by a bottle of Black or Red Label Whiskey. Those who had bad luck with the cards the night before ordered Teachers Whiskey!
The Greek food was very authentic and so tasty, that the regulars from the Greek Café (alleged gambling den) started to

bring along their mistresses. The word spread and non-gamblers started to arrive, first with their mistresses and then with their wives. Then "respectable" customers followed.
The Shalalie was taken off the wall and brought home. We kids would then play "restaurant owner and drunk bastards."
We would take it in turns to be the beaten up drunk bastard.

My dad's first restaurant was the only restaurant in North London to offer the famous Greek Meze.
The Greek Meze is a selection of cold dips, followed by a fish course and then a meat course. The final serving would be a tray of seasonal fruit and Greek coffee.

At the back of the restaurant, cooking some meals and preparing the dishes my mother made, was Whiplash – the Chef.
I won't mention his real name, just in case he is still working in the catering industry at the age of ninety nine!
My brother named him Chef Whiplash because the chef always had a runny nose. My brother says he often saw the chef grip his runny nostrils with thumb and forefinger and nasal blow into them. He would see the chef flick the snot on the kitchen floor. Big brother reckons he heard a whip crack as the snot sped through the air just before hitting the floor. It was also said that Whiplash would sometimes miss the floor and there was concern that his snot ended up in the Chef's special. Kind of ironic really!
Whiplash was old even for the seventics. His chef's jacket and apron were always covered in stains and once he slung a dirty

tea-towel over his shoulder it would remain stuck there till somebody with two hands was able to peel it off.
As well as Chef Whiplash, I remember the guy who washed the dishes who said he was the other son of God.
There was also the waitress whose name my mother often shouted out during arguments with the old man.

The dishwasher called himself Agios – which is the Greek name for Saint. He was a short guy with long flowing white hair. He had gold rings with precious stones on each finger and carried (almost a different one a week) the largest short-wave radio box- which for the 1970s (a decade before the boom-box made its debut) was implausible considering how many months wages those machines would have cost a washer of dishes – son of God or not.
He also wore real fur coats and often the waitress would beg him to loan her any one of his fur coats for the day.
This guy was a legend of The Seven Sisters Road in the seventies and sadly many years later, we heard that he was robbed of all his possessions, which really did send him over the edge then.
He once performed an exorcism on me. I didn't know what an exorcism was – he just told me and big brother that he will rid the devil from me after I once again tied the bottom leg openings of his overalls, so that when he tried to put them on, his leg would stumble on the knotted end and he would go arse-over-tit.

Pranks aside, I was of some help.

Big brother and I would go to the restaurant after school and help sweep up and then mop up prior to opening. Later, we would run home, pick up carrier bags containing trays or bowls of whatever homemade dishes my mum had prepared and take them back to the restaurant.

With a bag in each hand and a bag handle cutting into each of our palms, my brother and I would head back to the shop.

I would stop every fifty paces to swap bags over to different hands. Often I would stop for a breather before I would commence the half mile walk. Big brother would call out for me to keep up.

One day, one of the bags split at the bottom. The hot bowl containing stuffed vine-leaves hit the floor and some of the rolled vine-leaves unravelled leaving mincemeat and rice all over the pavement. I stood there with tears in my eyes. Big brother ended up carrying one of my bags as well as his two, while I held the hot bowl with two hands and with juice running down them.

We would return home again, this time with all the dirty tea-towels and table-cloths.

Before the day was over, one of us would go to Hornsey Road Laundry and Baths with mum for a late evening of boredom and sheet-folding in sweltering conditions due to all the heat coming out of the endless rows of washing machines and dryers.

On one evening a week, there would be no shortage of volunteers to go with mum to buy the ingredients to make all the Greek food for the restaurant. For a poor family in a poor neighbourhood (I should say ex-poor neighbourhood since most of the town houses are now worth over a million pounds), the food budget for the restaurant made our visits to the butchers and greengrocers a popular one with the traders. Mum would spend ten times the total of what the average household spent. That meant we kids would get ten times the amount of the Green Shield stamps.

Green Shield stamps were the 1970s equivalent of today's store reward cards. Like Club Card points, except Green Shield stamps were worth collecting and had monetary value, whereas most stores' Club Cards aint worth dick!
For every pound you spent, you'd get forty small Green Shield stamps. For households that spent many pounds, the merchant would issue the larger Green Shield stamp which was worth forty of the smaller stamps. The stamps would be stuck in special books issued by the Green Shield stamp shop and once a book was completed, you could redeem completed books for goods out of the Green Shield stamp catalogue.
As luck would have it, there was a Green Shield store opposite my dad's restaurant in the Seven Sisters Road.
Once mum chose the household items from the catalogue she wanted to trade completed books for, my siblings and I would end up with a few books to exchange for toys. On one occasion big brother and I exchanged a few completed stamp books for a stamp book and stamps! That annoyed and confused my mum. We had to explain that everyone collected world stamps. She didn't get it! She also didn't get the time I bought play money with real money!

* * *

The new restaurant

-was a double fronted one hundred covers Greek restaurant with live Bouzouki music on the weekends.
Bouzoukia! A place to listen to the Bouzouki whilst fine dining.
A bouzouki is a string instrument from Greece. It looks like a mandolin, but makes a much better sound when playing Rebetika!
Rebetika or Rebetiko is the name for the now popular urban Greek music which has its origins in the 1950s dockside bars and taverns of Greece. Greek ladies of the night loved to dance to the Rebetiko and Greek men would love to pay for their pleasure.

The restaurant was open plan. Most tables had a view straight into the kitchen. The first thing diners would notice was the large charcoal grill which almost ran the length of the entire kitchen. Above the charcoal grill, slow turning on a spit was the Souvla - large cuts of marinated lamb, slow cooking above the hot coals. The Souvla was served during the meat course of the Greek Meze. No surprise, once customers walked in and saw the meat turning and juices running off it, they would discard the menu and order the Meze.

The ceiling in my dad's restaurant was painted dark blue with a hundred silver stars stencilled on. When the diners looked up, they would get the feeling they were eating alfresco.

Bespoke paintings of Aphrodite (the Greek Goddess of love) adorned most walls and the signs to the ladies' and gents' toilets were of a Spartan warrior and a Greek maiden in a white toga.

The tables were rectangular bar one – a round table taking centre stage for VIPs.

I hated that table!

The staff had to sucker-up and kiss-arse, waiting the VIP table that historically proved to be the worst table for tips and the hardest to please.

On weekends, the staff numbered on average eleven including dad, plus my brother and I – provided we hadn't fallen out with dad for one reason or another.

There was a head-chef and two station chefs. A dishwasher (human not appliance) who also took out the bins and fed a chained up Tarzan's replacement!

And finally, five waiters, including the head-waiter and a barman or barmaid.

Big brother would be front of house covering tables whose waiter nipped out for a fag break.

I would be kept away from customers by helping out in the kitchen or behind the bar.

My favourite role was helping out at the Meze cold station where in one evening, I could peel and eat fifty fresh prawns dipped in a prawn cocktail sauce. When we were running low on prawns, I would help myself to the Scottish smoked salmon

Waiter staff turnover was quite high as dad insisted on professionalism with zero errors.

The waiter who holds the shortest employment record was an Egyptian guy, who in one night, waiting the same table, manged to spill not one, but two hot Irish coffees over the same poor lady, dressed to the nines, out with her husband on their anniversary.
When the first Irish coffee went all over her, dad went ape-shit and stepped in before the lady's husband could clobber the waiter. The guy was subdued with the announcement that any drinks thereafter were on the house.
You could see it coming a mile off as the Egyptian waiter nervously took the replacement Irish coffee over. When the second coffee hit the table and splashed her blouse once more, dad briefly allowed the husband to grab the waiter by the tie, but as to not upset the rest of the evening for the other customers, said guy was calmed with the promise that his entire meal including all drinks were on the house.

Kitchen staff had the longest employment time. For dad, the business was all about the food. Good chefs were hard to come by and once dad found a good one, they would be looked after financially and treated respectfully.
Dad often employed a down-on-his-luck fellow as a dishwasher-come dog trainer. Dad would pay them a good rate and allow them to have a good meal at the end of the shift. Once on their feet and ready to move on, another guy who'd hit hard times would fill the vacancy.

I can't help but admire the old man for what he achieved – business-wise that is. The place was a huge success and made....
Not sure if I should say – *it made the family a shitload of money*, or – *made my dad a shitload of money....*
Regardless - the place was a huge success. He would often say, especially after a bottle of German white wine, that he wasn't building up the business for himself, but for all his kids.
<One day sons, this will all be yours.>

When big brother and I were working, we would often disappoint my father one way or another. So dad would get the Bouzouktsis (one who plays the Bouzouki and can have any seedy woman he wants) to play and sing a Greek song called Gie Mou, which translates as Son of Mine.
The lyrics (roughly translated) went something like –
< My son, what are you waiting for, tell me,
My son, you didn't listen to your poor father,
My son, think of my pain,
My son, you will always be like a rootless tree, without destiny, without sun and sky,
My Son, my son, tell me what you want my son.>
Anyway you get the message...and so did we....every week!
Here –enjoy. This is the best version I can find on Youtube close to what we endured.
Put 8GB22bRK1I0 in the Youtube search bar if you dare... Or visit this book's accompaniment on Facebook by searching Sociably Awkward Frying Pan!

One night big brother was waiter-ing (waiting on tables) and I was behind the bar, hiding from the masses.
I don't know what possessed the Bouzouktsis (one who plays the Bouzouki and thinks he is the dog's bollocks), but he started playing and singing his rendition of Bésame Mucho to a packed house.
My brother and I looked at each other. There was a pause of ten seconds while the song sunk in and then we both burst out laughing.
There was no warning. There was no intro.
The songs starts immediately with...
"Bésame,
Bésame mucho."
In Spanish it means "kiss me a lot."
The Beatles did a cover which sounded as funny as the Bouzouktsis's version. One was sang in a Liverpudlian accent and the other in a Greek accent!
The Greek Bouzouktsis was so up his own arse that he didn't recognise that "mucho" is Greek Cypriot slang for "wank!"
"Bésame" is Greek for "we played."
In the Greek Cypriot dialect, we say "paisi mucho" when one masturbates. The literal translation is "plays wanking" meaning he's a wanker!
I know.....what a load of childish nonsense and I would agree. But it didn't stop my brother and I collapsing in fits of hysterics. It didn't stop us sign language-ing the wanker sign behind the Bouzouktsis's back.
Dad spotted us and got annoyed with both of us. He sent us home on a busy night when it became clear that we couldn't

compose ourselves. He told the geezer never to sing that song again in English, Greek or Spanish.

* * *

Sundays bloody (steak) Sundays.

The new restaurant was open seven evenings a week.
There were many dress factories and offices within a half mile radius and dad saw that there were no decent eateries for the lunchtime business men. So he started opening at lunchtimes on weekdays and Saturdays.
Staff numbers increased and cleaners were hired to clean before the lunchtime rush and before evening opening times. The cleaners had Sunday off, so I volunteered (for the going rate) to go to the restaurant on Sunday afternoons, to clear up the mess left behind after the late Saturday night trade and to prepare for Sunday evening opening.
I gave up my Sundays for selfish reasons. It was a chance to be alone for a few hours. And there was a cigarette machine and the key to it was in the till.
A few weeks into this new role and Sundays were living-like-a-king day!
I would arrive at just after midday. I would clear the tables of any plates and glasses left behind the previous Saturday night. Dad had this policy of never closing or chucking out anybody if they were spending money and having a good time. This meant that by four in the morning, only a few staff would stay behind whilst the majority clocked off. Whatever was on the

tables when the last of the diners decided to call it an evening stayed on the tables!

After washing the plates and glasses I would then lay new clean tablecloths, napkins and cutlery.
Before I got the Hoover out (all vacuum cleaners were called Hoovers), I would open (set-alight) the charcoal – a skill in itself. During the "hoovering" I would often find loose change or cigarette lighters and anything not of too high value would go into the lost-and-found pockets of my second hand army jacket (a jacket I loved but had to give up after I met my missus).
When the "hoovering" was over and the restaurant was spick and span, I would go into "Pasha" mode!

"Pasha" was one of my dad's favourite words. A Pasha was a high ranking official or general in the Ottoman Empire.
One of the restaurant's longest serving chefs was a Turkish guy. Dad would often pull his leg.
One quiet night, my dad called all the staff to the kitchen and told us all the story of a Pasha who went to invade the Island of Malta on behalf of the Ottoman Empire.
The Ottoman Pasha led a flotilla of ships through the Mediterranean in search of Malta. Two weeks after leaving port, the Pasha calls his men to the captain's cabin and says, "Today we invade Malta." (Yep, I'm using speech marks for this as these are not my memories but a well-known fable amongst us late night Greeks)!

The Pasha lays out the nautical maps on his table and places his hands down stopping the map from rolling up.
"Malta," the Pasha says looking down at the map. "Malta, Malta, Malta......Malta?"
The Pasha couldn't find The Island of Malta on the map. He turns to his men and they all shrug.
One of his men notices that the Pasha has placed his thumb over where the Island of Malta is, but fearing beheading for embarrassing the Pasha, he says nothing.
Two months at sea and eventually the Pasha has no choice but to set sail back to Turkey.
The Pasha is called before the Emperor.
"What news?" The Emperor asks.
"My Lord," the Pasha says, "Malta Yok!"

"Var" in Turkish means "there is."
"Yok" in Turkish means "there is not."
<*Malta Yok.*> We would cry out as the Turkish chef chased us with a butcher's chopper.

By the time I finished the "hoovering", the charcoal would be white-hot. I would then go into the cold store and select the thickest sirloin steak with a good trim of fat.
Although a fillet steak was a better cut of meat, I preferred the sirloin because of its fat content.
On the charcoal, a sirloin steak cooked to medium-rare with a bloodied middle section would only take two minutes either side.

So five minutes later, I was sat at the round VIP table with a half pint of draught Carlsberg and a large plate containing a sirloin steak seeping blood.
Ten minutes later, I was on my second cigarette.

* * *

A short story about another Sunday.

An observation rather than a tale.
It was one Sunday afternoon. Not too long after the Brixton riots of 1981 triggered sporadic copy-cat micro riots in London and beyond.
I was sat on the VIP table finishing of a steak. Something catches my eye and as I look up from the table towards the front windows, I can see a myriad of flashing blue and white lights. I get up and approach the front door. I look out and take in the spectacle. On the opposite footpath there is a large gathering of youths stretching back almost towards the Hornsey Road and onward past the restaurant towards Finsbury Park. It seemed like the restaurant was at the epicentre of what was about to kick off.
In the middle of the road was a fleet of emergency vehicles. Most were police vans.
I rushed to the coin-operated phone. Then I rushed to the till and grabbed a ten pence coin and went back to the phone.

I called my dad at home and described the situation. He tells me to lock the front door (which was already locked), close all the lights and he will be there soon.
Twenty-five minutes later I see my dad approach the door.
I then see him have a quick chat to one of the police officers.
I then see a group of youths point towards my dad and that scares the shit out of me.
My father taps on the glass door and I let him in.
<*You've been smoking*?>He says to me.
<*No dad, it's probably from last night. I've kept the windows closed because of outside.....forget that. What are we going to do?*>
Some of the staff start arriving and dad tells then to forget about opening up the restaurant today.
The noise levels outside start building up and the sky is darkening with the approaching dusk and impeding storm.
For a while there's a stalemate- with youths on one side and coppers on the other waiting for the youths to move on or make a move.

It kicks off.
Some youths split out in all directions and others start throwing stones. The police give chase and my dad tells us all to move into the kitchen at the rear.
For twenty minutes, sirens are blazing and youths are shouting and swearing. Glass bottles and windows are being smashed and I can hear banging and screaming.
It could have been more than twenty minutes or less. I'm just guessing today, but then it seemed like it went on for ages.

It starts to quieten outside, but the flashing emergency lights illuminate the inside of the restaurant.
My dad leads and we follow him towards the front. A quick look out the window tells my father that the mini-riot is either over or has moved on. He opens the door and we all go outside for a look.
I was right about hearing broken glass as the shops either side of us has all had their windows smashed in. The off-licence next door has its door off its hinges with smashed crates of beer and spirit bottles scattered around its shop-front. All shops along our block are showing damage of one sort or another. The bookies seems to have borne the brunt!
The only premises unscathed is my father's restaurant.
<*Nobody's going to come out for a meal tonight, we might as well go home,*> my dad tells the staff, <*but let's eat first!*>
<*I could do with a fag.*> I say, getting back a disapproving look from dad!

* * *

The first love of my life:- Part 1

Since I met the first love of my life in the restaurant, it seemed appropriate that I leave the saga in the restaurant chapter.
It's not like I had many loves that I could have created the Love Chapter! No, Alexia belongs here....

I was sixteen and Alexia was forty-three.
Alexia was from Greece, the motherland and she was mysterious and attractive, with large dark eyes and a large chest. She wore low cut tops with a cleavage you can park a Chopper bike in. She could have passed for twenty-three with her long eye lashes and bright red lips. She spoke with an accent which made her sound vulnerable, then you would notice her cleavage again and think - with a bosom like that, the vulnerable ones were the poor sods she made eyes at.
She had a nice smell. A scent of flowers and sweets – the flying saucer ones filled with sherbet.
I wouldn't have a clue what the name of that perfume was and why would you care? All I can see is that damn cleavage and that line coming down from neck to somewhere behind that blouse. A cleavage that Moses could not part. A cleavage that Evel Knievel would fail to jump. A cleavage for all mankind..........a cleavage that could launch a thousand ships and a fleet of Ford Capris.
You'd forgive me for going on if you had seen the Cleave..... unless you're my wife reading this, which in that case, I shall move on with the story.....but fear not my sweet.....it's me we're talking about, so the story will end badly!

I had just finished my O'levels and was on a long summer break working at my dad's restaurant. At the end of this stint, I would decide my future.
They were fully staffed in the kitchen - a position that I loved working at – away from people. So on this shift, I was working behind the bar.

The bar also suited me fine because I hated serving customers or being customer facing in any way.
This was a bar where customers could not approach. It was a bar where the waiters would shout out the drinks orders on the way to the kitchen and I would have the drinks prepared on their way back out to the floor.
The bar and the spirit bottles behind me were visible to the whole house, so I had to dress smart with a shirt and tie.
As long as I didn't look up over the floor area, or make eye contact with any customers, then I was capable and more than happy to work in this post. Even happier when Alexia turned up and I was told that she would be my replacement once or if I went back to school. All I had to do was train her and stack clean drink trays between her ample breasts.

FISHNETS!
Sorry, I just remembered that she also wore short skirts with bright fishnet stockings showing. If you were able to pull your eyes off her top, they would only land on those hypnotic legs where the patterns on those fishnets sent you in a trance.
So there I was, sixteen years old, on a Friday evening - an hour and a half before the rush and in walked Alexia.

It's at this part of the story that some of you amateur psychologists would bring up Sigmund Freud's Oedipus Complex. Well let me tell you guys straight. I had no desire for a sexual relationship with a parent of the opposite sex, nor was I jealous of the same sex parent! I attended family counselling for a few weeks and I came to the conclusion that all

psychologists were stoned. My mum looked nothing like Alexia. The only thing they had in common was age...oh and possibly cleavage but I feel sick just mentioning this.
Let me tell you that I deleted and re-inserted the above line several times. I decided to keep it in as proof that I have nothing to fear about the rantings of an Austrian-German who died nearly a hundred years ago. A time when incest was the norm.
So now that the elephant in the room has been shoved well and truly in the corner, I can get back to my first love.

In walked Alexia. A cross between the singer Cher, Marie Osmond, Saint Mother Teresa of Calcutta and Chesty Morgan. She was wearing a bright yellow top, a short skirt and orange fishnet tights. One of the waiters said she resembled Sesame Street's Big Bird. She sauntered towards the rear with her rear swaying side to side. Her tits were hard boiled ostrich eggs.

A waiter once asked me if I preferred fried or boiled eggs? I said scrambled and he laughed. He then explained the meaning of his question – do you like big tits on a girl or flat chested girls?

My dad introduced Alexia to the staff in order of rank. She shook hands with the head waiter, and then to the four other waiters, followed by the waiter who couldn't speak Greek or English so his role was to pick up the dirty glasses and plates and to make sure the ashtrays were emptied regularly. Dad then leads Alexia past the bar towards the kitchen and she

shakes hands with the head chef, the assistant chef and the guy who cuts the salads and fruits and assembles the cold dishes for the Greek Meze. She even stops and shakes hands with Hadji, our Turkish washer-uppa. Finally, dad leads her back towards the bar and introduces me – head and only barman.
We shook hands.

Looking back now, I can only assume that Alexia was a raving lunatic or a sexual deviant. Back then though, she was everything a sixteen year old could ever wish for.
By the end of the first week, she told me I had beautiful, deep-thinking eyes that held all manner of mysteries. The only thing my eyes held then were the images of each of her breasts burnt into each of my retinas.
By the second week, she was touching my arm and rubbed against me as she passed by me behind the narrow drinks bar. She would whisper sexual compliments and would ask me if I held feelings for her. One feeling was obvious as I had to constantly face forwards towards the counter so that I could hide the embarrassing bulge.
My old wanking sock was able to stand on its own by week three.
By week four she was given her notice to leave. Man did that cause a rift between my father and me.

My dad, the waiters, the chef and his assistant, some regulars and even Hadji had noticed the inappropriate interactions between me and Alexia. They noticed that I wasn't getting any

of the drinks orders right and that I had a dopey look on my face. On top of that, Alexia was the worst barmaid the restaurant had employed.
I fell out with the head waiter when I caught him flirting with my Alexia. I squared up to him, chest puffed out and fists clenched, but he walked away laughing after he told me that he completed his commando training during his two years in the Cypriot National Guard.
<*So you learnt to make Greek coffee then*!> was my excellent retort to his macho remark.

My dad took me to one side and told me to pull my socks up – which was difficult as I was running out of clean socks. Well I couldn't put them in the wash basket in the state they were in! I accused my dad of being jealous. I said all manner of things. If any good came of it, well that was seeing my mother and father agreeing that my behaviour was humiliating the family and the business and that Alexia had to be given her notice.
They both sat me down and for the first time ever, I was given a dual parental lecture (told you there was good to be found).
The lecture was about Pantellis the only Greek Cypriot road-sweeper in Islington, London, England. He also provided the restaurant with large black bin bags which Hadji would turn inside-out to hide the large white embossed letters – L.B ISLINGTON.
Apparently, Pantellis was infamous amongst the Holloway Greek Cypriot community and back home in Cyprus where the story (lecture) starts.

Please allow me to stick the following into a sub-chapter as I may one day copy it into my next book – a prequel to The Holloway Years.

* * *

The Cyprus years:- Pantellis story

Cyprus (around the) 1950s......

Pantellis was tall, athletic and the most handsome young man in the village. It was said that he never partook in any bestiality which was not uncommon in certain villages.

There was a neighbouring village story about a youth who took over from his sick father taking their olive oil to market. During the journey, the son would steer the donkey and cart off track and take him behind a large tree in a field where he would then proceed to take the donkey from behind – donkey style.

When the father got better and started taking his goods to market, the donkey insisted on going off road and made his own way to the large tree. Once there, the donkey wouldn't budge.

Erm...anyway........

Pantellis was a labourer. He could not be anything but a labourer, because as the old Cypriot proverb goes, "give a donkey a brain and he will take advantage of his foot-long knob!"

Pantellis was also the village fool, the brunt of practical jokes and preyed upon by the all in the village, especially my maternal grandfather.

Pantellis's parents were at the end of their tether (or in Cypriot terms – end of their worry beads). Other families were marrying sons and daughters off whilst gaining land and livestock. The local matchmaker had no such luck with Pantellis though. He would attend the Proxenia and the girl and her families' eyes would light up.....until he spoke!
Proxenia is the old Cypriot custom for arranging marriages. Either two families would get together on their own accord to introduce their children to each other, or they would employ the services of the village busy-body. Dowries would be discussed and hands shaken. And if there was any semblance of attraction between the couple, all the better for it. They will have loving grandchildren. If not, then tough shit in certain cases.
At twenty years of age, Pantellis's parents were losing all hope of finding a wife/daughter-in-law. They exhausted searches in their and neighbouring villages.
When all seemed lost and Pantellis's parents were to be stuck with the large oaf, he caught the eye of Panayiota – the village twice-widowed spinster.

Yeah I know, a widow cannot be a spinster....but they can in Cyprus!

Panayiota was a semi-unattractive childless late-forty year old. During her two marriages she had accumulated some wealth. As she approached fifty, the likelihood of finding another man was non-existent.

Can you see where this story/lecture is going...? Am I the oaf?

To cut a long story short (I may want to extend it for the prequel) Pantellis and Panayiota were married. Pantellis's parents insisted and without the prospect of any future grandchildren, they settled for a herd of goats and some chickens.
It wasn't all bad though. By all accounts, Pantellis was having good sex....in the dark.

During the intercommunal violence taking place in Cyprus at that time, Panayiota and Pantellis decided to follow some of the other folk and move to England, lock, stock and two tin-barrels of freshly made halloumi.

England was the land of opportunity for poor immigrants. But when you were a wealthy twenty year old stud with an aging wife and you visit the bright lights of London - well the bars, side-street casinos and prostitutes could not hold back Pantellis.

Jump forward to 1979.
Pantellis gambled all of his wife's fortune and is now sweeping the streets and selling plastic bin bags on the side. He goes home to an old bedridden woman twice his age.
<Is that how you want to end up son?>

* * *

The first love of my life:- Part 2

<*But I'm not Pantellis,*> I shouted.

Not sure if my parents were overreacting or perhaps they saw where this harmless flaunting was heading. Actually it wasn't flaunting...I was besotted. When they saw that the lecture hadn't sunk into my immature brain, they decided on another proven course of action. They booked me a plane flight to Cyprus.

Turns out, they needn't have gone through all that bother. I am more than capable of saying the wrong things, or acting like a total dick.

Half an hour alone with Alexia and she said her goodbyes for good.

On her last day at work, Alexia arranged that I should meet her the following week. She said she would pick me up outside The Rainbow in Seven Sisters Road as I couldn't make my own way to her address in Palmers Green (or as it is known today – Palmers Greece due to the amount of Greek Cypriots living there).

That week I was a mental wreck. I couldn't eat or sleep.

Does she intend to er.....you know...seduce me?

Throughout school I often dreamt about being propositioned by one of the female French teachers and here I was, about to meet a sexual forty year old with tits that could crack a crab shell.

I've never had a girlfriend let alone been in a position where I was to cop-a-feel and some!

I tried talking to my older brother, and all he could say was <*Take an extra pair of clean pants with you!*>

The O'level results were out soon, but I couldn't even consider my future beyond the next week. That effing Pantellis story played on my mine too. Yeah she was hot, but do I really want to end up sweeping the streets....
WHAT ARE YOU WORRIED ABOUT PAN?? This is what boys my age dream of. Shit, this is what men of any age dream of.
Sod Pantellis....I'm going.

Dressed in jeans and a cool leather bomber jacket, I stood outside The Rainbow theatre on the corner of Seven Sisters Road and Isledon Road. Even before she turned up, I had a stirring in my nutsack. Luckily the bomber jacket was one size too big and I was able to hide my crotch with both hands in either side pockets pulled down over my groin area.
It was mid-summer and I was starting to sweat from the heat and anticipation.
I saw her Ford Cortina turn into Isledon Road and continue for another fifty metres till she found a space to pull into.
I initially went to run, then found that I couldn't, so I calmly walked towards her car. She saw me in the rear view mirror and leaned over to the passenger side and lifted up the doors' locking mechanism.
With my right hand still in the jacket's side pocket, I casually opened the car door with my left and struggled to sit in the passenger seat without bending my penis.
<*Hello Alexia.*> I say drooling.

<*Hello Pani.*> She says turning in the driver's seat to face me.
To this day I hate being called "Pani".
Here we are. Alone. And I'm shitting a brick!
<*I missed you.*> I say in a deep, dumbass voice which sounds a lot like Mongo from the film Blazing Saddles.
<*I missed you too Pani.*>
I ready myself. I've seen Roger Moore in Live and Let Die and now is the time to seduce like Roger does.
I unsteadily move my right arm over and rest it on top of her seat. If she had just leaned forward a bit, I could have had my arm across her shoulders, but this will have to do.
I slowly look at her legs. She has a short skirt on but no fishnets. I notice a few veins that weren't there the last time I looked. I move up to her top and YES, nothing has changed there.
<*Shall we go for a drive*?> she says in her perfect seductive Greek accent.
I didn't immediately respond. I was still staring at her top.
The sweat was running down my back and my pants were about to take the full force of a Greek volcano eruption.
By the way, according to Wikipedia, "*in 1646 BC a massive volcanic eruption, perhaps one of the largest ever witnessed by mankind, took place at Thera (present day Santorini), an island in the Aegean not far from Crete*".

My mind started to wander. I was stalling – delaying what was about to be the greatest moment of my life.
I saw flashes of my parents and Pantellis pushing Panayiota in her wheelchair.

I swiftly pushed all non-sexual thoughts out of my mind and looked up at Alexia. She looked different in sunlight. I was used to looking at her with the blue-tinged mood lighting my dad had installed in his restaurant. That afternoon, she was caked in makeup.
She leans forward and says <*well?*>
I leaned forward.
And I say...............the first thing that came to my lips.
<*If you didn't have all that lipstick on, I would kiss you.*>

I was walking home sixty seconds later. Kicking myself.
She made up some excuse that she had to pay her landlord her rent money. She kicked me out and drove off.

I arrived home and made a dash for my bedroom. I was thoroughly depressed and all I wanted to do was change into my pyjamas, lie on my bed and go to sleep.
I emptied my jean pockets of house keys and loose change.
Then I pulled out my spare pair of clean pants from my bomber jacket and put them back in the bottom draw. I never saw Alexia again.

CHAPTER 14:-CYPRUS, THE ISLAND OF APHRODITE

If anyone needed a holiday more than me, it was my parents. Preferably separate holidays. They needed a break from each other, from the business, from the housework, the stress, the fighting, from us kids. They never had a holiday. They never went away as a couple. They never had a day off. They never came to England together. They arrived separately.
They only had kids together!

It would have been something though if they did go away together. A romantic break just the two of them. Then they'd return with gifts for us kids and tell us about some amusing mishap that happened. Mum getting tipsy or dad losing his trunks in the sea and mum having to escort him out of the sea with her towel wrapped around him.
Life would begin again for them. It wouldn't be too late. Many middle aged couples start all over. Dad would install a manager then eventually leave the business to one or all of his kids to run. Whichever of us was willing, or able, or willing and able!
With the money the business was making, my parents would build a modern house in Cyprus, next door to the old stone house they spent their first night as a couple in.
They would retire from work and spend six months in the UK and six months in Cyprus. We kids would be socially (or sociably) apt.

During the school holidays there would be these big family gatherings and we would sit outside, around a large wooden table built around a two hundred year old olive tree.
Their grandchildren would spend the summer holidays with them and my parents would spoil them rotten.
Then late one night I would get a phone call. It would be my mother telling me that my father was not well. My siblings and I would immediately book our flights online and the next morning we would be in Cyprus, standing around my father's sick-bed.
<*Don't worry about the restaurant.*> Big brother would tell our father.
<*The business is doing fine. The new menu little brother introduced is a big success. You just concentrate on getting better.*>
And dad would smile and nod while mum held her husband's hand.
<*Don't worry mum.*> My sisters would say. <*We are here now.*>

I was sixteen when they booked my flights.
What would they need a holiday for? They were either happy with the status quo or knew no other life – no alternate reality!
My parents insisted that I went. They wanted to put some distance between me and Alexia. They were either worried that I would bring shame on the family or concerned that I was going to ruin my life. They needn't worry because I had managed to put Alexia behind me the second day after she kicked me out of her car. I was resolute. My feelings or emotive state was such that one shrug and life could move on. It's that easy for me.

I had a passport ready for a school skiing trip that I never attended. Actually, I was excluded from that trip due to my behaviour. I ask you!
It was my first holiday. It was my first trip to Cyprus. My first trip anywhere.
I was to accompany my aunt and uncle on their annual Cypriot getaway. My uncle (my dad's sister's husband) was working at my dad's restaurant at the time. He was a good guy and had a good sense of humor, so I didn't object to going with them.
We were to stay with his family who lived in a small village three miles from Larnaca and only one mile from the beach.
When the time approached, I was looking forward to it.
When my dad gave me a hundred pounds to spend as I saw fit, I wished I was there yesterday.
When my dad gave me the money, he winked and said, <*Enjoy yourself, know what I mean?*> I didn't, but I think I did at a later date.
It could have been a coincidence or pre-arranged, nevertheless, but I was put in a situation where "enjoy" didn't come in to it. I'll get to that part later......

The first thing that hit me was the heat and humidity.
We landed in Larnaca airport and when the cabin crew opened the plane's door and that heat and steam rushed in, my hair frizzed and my pubes straightened.
As I walked down the mobile stairway in the August afternoon sun - I had never experienced heat like it.

When you're an ugly git like me, you leave your hair long so that it can cover your big ears and make your big nose look smaller. By the time my foot left the last step and I stood on the tarmac, my hair looked like one of the seventies Harlem Globetrotter's afro. Sweat was running down my neck and down my crotch. I was dressed for Holloway – denim jeans, Adidas sweatshirt (which wasn't a shirt but a flipping jumper. The sweat part was correct though) and a cool looking leather jacket – which started to smell like a dead cow left out to rot. We had summers in Holloway, but this was Johnny Storm (The Human Torch) *flame-on* hot.
Bollocks, I should have gone to dad's barber.

I staggered over to the immigration desk and was delayed by a Cypriot officer with a gun. He wouldn't let me through at first as I looked nothing like my passport picture. My uncle had to vouch for me and explain that I was not a member of the Palestinian militant group (The PLO) and that I was sweating profusely not because I was planning to hijack a plane, but because I was a Charlie.
<*Charlis? Ah, entaxi*> he said, and eventually let me through.
A Charlie is a belittling name given to English-born-Cypriot-males by Cyprus-born-Cypriots.
Charlie...as in Prince Charles.
Charlou is the feminine name for English-born-Cypriots.
Kolo-tripa is Greek for arsehole. And once I was out of range of his firearm, I called him that.

Although my mother tongue is Greek with a heavy Cypriot dialect, I never got round to speaking it much. To be honest, barring all Greek Cypriot swear words, my vocabulary in my mother tongue was/is pretty poor.
Whilst on the subject and since some of you guys paid good money to download and read my autobiography (instead of Katie Price's or one of the Beckham kids), I thought I'd compensate you with a quick guide to some classic Cypriot swear phrases you can use at Larnaca Airport...then I can move on to the rest of this chapter.

<*Vre Gaurospore, pontes valitses mou?*> Oi donkey sperm, where is my luggage?
<*Balestinian ego? Gamo tin ratsa sou.*> Me a Palestinian? I screw your family (can also mean their whole heritage).
<*Ston kolo sou repani vre taxigi.*> Shove a radish up your arse Mr. taxi-driver (this one loses something in translation.
<*Na fkallis fausa!*> Shut the fuck up!

We waited at the baggage carousel for hours. I wanted to go home. There was no aircon. I didn't know what aircon was anyway. I was dying from the heat. I was delirious with thirst. I was willing to give the hundred pounds my dad gave me for a McDonald's fifty percent ice, fifty percent coke drink.
Where the fuck is the sea?
The terminal was part built at that time and if you looked around the side of the carousel machinery, you would see the airport workers sitting on a pile of suitcases smoking and eating bread with black olives.

I gave my uncle a nod towards them with a what-the-fuck look and he shrugged and said, <*This is Cyprus, get used to it.*>
A further hour past. We had our luggage and we were finally on our way to the village, courtesy of my uncle's father who picked us up in a motor which had a top speed of twenty three miles an hour.

We arrived in the village of Aradippou or as we Charlies call it – Harry-dipped-in-the-poo. Not only a play on the name of the village but also in reference to how the village smells due to the numerous pig farms that surround it.
I'll refrain from mocking the place because of the hospitality I received from my uncle's parents. They had a modest sized bungalow with many ground floor additions and steel reinforcement bars sticking out the roof. The steel bars were for any future first floor builds that would complete the house thus qualifying for exemption from property tax.
My uncle's siblings had their own houses nearby, so I got a room all to myself.
This place was to be our base, my home for the next three weeks with a week planned away at my grandparents whom I never met before. That should be interesting.

I couldn't sleep that night. The heat was unbearable. I was still thirsty after I had drank a gallon of water at dinner time.
That was another first, sitting outdoors eating whilst people walked by. As they passed the house, they would be invited by our hosts to come up to the veranda and be introduced to the visitors from England.

For the locals, less than a decade after the Turkish Invasion, all returning Cypriots and Charlies were rich and successful. Even me. Before the evening came to an end, I was offered the hand of three local girls to marry. One guy said he was going to go home immediately and fetch his daughter, but my uncle managed to persuade him that it had been a long day and I was very tired and that there was plenty of time for introductions. <*They do know I'm only sixteen yeah?*> I told my uncle. <*Beside, I need a flipping haircut first!*>
My uncle replies <*Wait when the locals find out your dad owns a restaurant in London, you'll be offered the good-looking ones too!*>

I tossed and turned and threw my pyjamas off and laid with just my sticky Y-fronts on. The room was dark. It was the darkest night I'd ever seen. Before I went to bed I looked up at the night sky and saw a million stars. In Holloway, we had around a dozen or so.
I couldn't get to sleep. I never experienced humidity before that day and I certainly never experienced a noise like the annoying sound that came from the other side of the window left wide open.
Earlier, I had tried to close and lock the window, but it wouldn't budge. I told my uncle about it and he laughed when I said I wanted it shut because of burglars. Now I know why he laughed. Burglars cruising the streets at night were driven mad at the constant chirping of crickets.
Just as I was drifting off, there was a low buzzing sound coming from inside the room. And then from inside one of my ears. <*What the fuck is this now?*>

When I woke up, I was covered in insect bites. <*Fucking mosquitoes.*> I was bitten everywhere. On my arms and legs, on my neck and behind my knee caps. Sometime during the night, my pants must have slipped down, because the bastards bit me on the arse cheeks too.
My hair was another thing. I looked like Trog from the seventies Sci-fi film called....Trog!
I got dressed and met my uncle for breakfast. I asked if he could take me to the barbers first thing. He said he would but I should be aware..... The barber is a relation of his and he has a daughter!

* * *

A visit to a brothel!

Nothing happened!
I REPEAT – NOTHING HAPPENED!
Now that's out of the way, I can continue with this sordid tale.
But first a joke
Please note: - Any resemblance to the play "Waiting for Godot" by Samuel Beckett is purely coincidental.
My big brother told me the following joke and as far as I am concerned Samuel Beckett is a character played by the famous actor Scott Bakula in the hit TV show – Quantum Leap.
This joke came to mind when I initially tried to write this sub-chapter. I didn't get it then, but half get it now. It reminds me of that day in Larnaca.

A guy goes to a brothel.

He pays his entrance fee and is led to a hallway with two doors.
One door has a sign saying Blondes and the other Brunettes.
He goes through the door marked Blondes and is immediately faced with two further doors and two further choices.
One door says Large Breasts and the other Small Breasts.
He goes through the Large Breasts door and again faces two more doors.
One door states Large Vagina and the other Small Vagina.
He steps through the door marked Large Vagina and finds himself back outside in the street!

During that first week, I went to the beach three times and spent a day up in the Troodos Mountains. My uncle introduced me to his younger cousin. He was eighteen years of age and exempt from National Service. He said it was due to his flat feet. My uncle told me later it was because of his heart condition he'd had since birth. By all accounts he was as healthy as anyone of us, but his parents being parents arranged his exemption with the help of a letter written by the family doctor. It was then that I was informed that as a sixteen year old Cypriot (regardless of where I was born) I should have arranged to get an exit-visa from the Cypriot Consulate in London as there was a chance that I may be conscripted on my departure. <*oh great!*>

One evening, we were at the local youth café/club playing pool and drinking coke. The cousin turns to me with a mischievous grin and asks me in Greek if I want to go and play <*Mappa*> (football) this Saturday?

In Cyprus, any relative of a relative is automatically your relative. If you buy some pigs from the farmer, the farmer is your relative. The barber who cut my hair and showed me a picture of his daughter asked me to call him uncle.

I look at the cousin, shrug and say noncommittally in Greek <*Football, yeah er...why not.*>

<*No Malaka.....Map-pa.*> He says and this time makes an O sign with his left hand and pokes at it with the middle digit of his right hand.

<*What the fuck are you doing?*> I snap back in Greek. I then revert back to English Cockney and say <*I aint no fucking perv you sad g-,*> but before I could finish the word "git" he comes up to me and whispers the words <No, *we go to the poutanes on Saturday.*>

Poutana is a derogatory Cypriot slang word for a lady who sells herself- a prostitute.

Poutanes is the plural.

In Cyprus, the word Poutana can also be used to describe a woman of relaxed moral values, not necessarily a prostitute.

I was taken aback by the suggestion. I've never had a proper girlfriend and now I was invited to go the whole way with an exotic lady whom I never met.

In hindsight I should have just said no. I should have made an excuse. But I was drawn to the notion of spending the night with a hot lady who would blow away the cobwebs and make a man out of me. To turn me from an awkward idiot with low self-esteem to a confident man about town.

I had the money my father gave me. It should be enough. Drinks, dinner, taxi and hotel room or if I'm lucky, back to her place to spend the night.
What would I say to my uncle when I wouldn't come home that night? I'll think of that later. I had other things to worry about, like what does this lady look like? Will she be a blonde or ginger, tall or short? I preferred short...I think.
My thoughts are interrupted by the cousin.
<*So, are we going to... you know?*> He says whilst he does that action with hands again.
I look around to make sure nobody is watching him shag his hand with his finger.
<*Okay let's do it.*> I say.

Saturday arrived. It followed another sleepless night. This time it wasn't the heat, or the crickets or the fear of somebody coming through the open window. It was anxiety that kept me up. Tonight was the night. A milestone in a boy's – correction – a man's life.
The day before, I asked the cousin a hundred questions.
<*Where are we going to meet them? What are they like? How much will they cost? Where do we get Gianakies (Johnnies) from?*>
There was one question I kept asking myself. <*What the hell am I doing? How the hell do I do it?*>
The cousin was vague. He never gave a straight answer to any of my questions.
If big brother was here, he'd know what to do. He'd be able to advise me. He'd done it plenty of times.

<*You never forget the day you lose your virginity!*> He told me once.
Well, I haven't forgotten that night and not because of what big brother had said either!

The cousin and I stood on the grassy knoll by the main road into town trying to hail a taxi (or to shoot Kennedy).
It was getting dark. Eventually one stopped and we both got in the back. The cousin calls out an address to the driver.
The driver shakes his head laughing.
I didn't catch on!
We reached the town. The driver then drove down the promenade with the beach and palm trees on one side and decorative street lights with restaurants and hotels on the other. I pulled my wallet out preparing to pay the driver when he stopped. But he didn't stop, he drove past the restaurants and bars. He drove past the hotels. I looked over to the cousin confused. He looked back with a grin. I was thankful that he didn't start simulating sex with his hands again.
The taxi driver reached the end of the promenade and turned right and continued down a dark tarmac road. Then he turned left down a dirt track.
I started to panic. I looked at the cousin and motioned a "what the fuck" action with both hands. The cousin motions "calm down" by waving an open hand downwards.
Two minutes later, the driver pulls over.

The previous day's excitement and trepidation gave way to sheer panic. The cousin opened his door and got out. Then he

leaned in and dragged me out. He nods at me and then at the driver. I pay the guy and he drives off.
We stand on a path. We are in an elevated position and I can see the town's lights to my left. I turn to my right and follow the path with my eyes up. I can make out a row of buildings. They look like sheds, but later I learn that they are prefabricated dwellings for refugees displaced after the Turkish Invasion.
I pat my trouser leg and feel the false assurance of the little pocket knife I purchased a few days back at a street kiosk. I'm ready to flee and the cousin can see the concern on my face. <*Don't worry Vre.*> He says <I*t's ok, you'll see.*>

We walk up the path towards the small one level buildings.
The whole place looks abandoned. Down at the end of the row, there's a vacant plot then a further two buildings. There is light coming from inside and I can see movement outside. We get closer and I can see figures outside smoking.
It's three young men dressed in army combat uniforms. They're young National Service men. Behind them I spot an old woman sitting on a wooden chair smoking a pipe.
No! I made that bit up – she was smoking a cigarette. I just let my mind wander there for a minute. But she did remind me of a picture I saw in a book once, of an old hag smoking a pipe.
I look at the cousin and I have a pleading look on my face which says "please let's go home".
Just then, behind the old lady, a door on the right of a pair of doors opens and out comes another young soldier, red-faced and beaming. His friends approach him chuckling and start

slapping his back. Standing by the door is a woman wearing a robe with a low frilly neck (stereotypical, I know...but true).
If this is the lady I've come to see then I am definitely out of here. She's as old as the barmaid I had a thing for (see, I'm over her already) but less attractive. A lot less attractive and plump. It's hot and her fringe is matted to her forehead.
<*I want to go home.*> There, I've gone and said it. I don't give a shit if I get abuse or ridiculed by the cousin or the soldiers who are sticking around. Then I realise why they haven't left. The other door opens and a younger man in jeans and a T-shirt comes out. He has his chest puffed out like he's won the Football Pools. He rushes to the awaiting soldiers and off they go laughing and slapping each other in the nuts.
The woman that follows him out is older than the first and uglier.

I repeated my plea, <*I want to go home.*>
<*Don't be a Pushti.*> the cousin replies. "Pushti" is Greek slang for homosexual. And with that he pushes me towards the old hag. The pimp!
Both ladies go inside their respective abodes.
The cousin taunts me and I have a choice. Either I punch him in the face and try and find my way out of here, forever to be known as the village Pushti, or I face this head-on like the man that I am intending to be. If going into that room proves that I am a man, then so be it.
<*You never forget the day you lose your virginity!*> My brother said.
Shit –this will be a day I would want to forget.
This is not what I expected.

The cousin is talking to the hag. Then its sounds like he is haggling. He turns to me and says <*Ten pounds.*>
Great – I won't be spending the night after all.
<*Which door do you wa...?*> and before he can finish his sentence, I make for the door on the right.

<*You never forget the day you lose your virginity!*>
I didn't lose my virginity that day.
For weeks and months after that night, my head was screwed instead!
I started to question my actions and my sexuality.
I find women attractive. I like girls. I like pictures of boobs and I'm always trying to get into X-rated movies at the Odeon with my mates. Hell, I've even got a deck of porno playing cards hidden in my sock draw. I often get them out and played Twenty-one...alone).
I found Alexia highly sexy. Had it not been for putting my foot in my mouth – who knows? But then, perhaps I bottled it. Why?

It's hard trying to describe my confused feelings back then when today I'm a married man with three kids with no doubts about my sexuality. Ok, I like musicals such as Seven Brides for Seven Brothers and West Side Story. I've seen Phantom of The Opera at the West End and I cried when Falcon Eddy killed Tom in the T.V mini-series Rich Man – Poor Man.
You can say that I am confident about my sexuality as well as being totally politically incorrect with my old ways. But there is no doubt - If I was socially inept before, then that trip to the brothel just cemented it. I am sociably inept!

I gave the cousin twenty Cypriot pounds (two ten pound notes) as I proceeded to walk through the door on the right. He gives the old hag ten pounds, pockets the other ten pounds (huh?) and walks through the door on the left.

The lady with the robe was sitting on the bed smoking.
There was a fan behind her blowing the smoke in my direction.
She indicated with her finger that she would be but a minute.
I looked around. The room was bare apart from the bed and a small black and white television mounted on a shelf at head height opposite the bed. There was a news or current affairs programme on with the volume turned down. I couldn't help but notice that the television was set at an angle and the screen would be visible to somebody laying on the bed....on her back!
I stood there silent. It felt wrong.
She stubbed her cigarette out.
I felt sorry for her. I was hot and I started to sweat. I felt bad. When she stood up and I saw half her backside when her robe opened, the room started to spin. I felt sick.
I ran out!

Seven minutes later, the cousin walked out with a grin wider than a Cheshire Cat's.
He gave me a questionable thumbs up......
I gave him an affirmative thumbs up back!
Under my breath I called him an arsehole!

* * *

The trip to Maroni.

The village of Maroni existed in medieval times. It was said that King Richard the Lionheart stopped at Maroni on a break from the crusades. It was also said that he had a fling with a Cypriot girl who bore his child out of wedlock. This girl secretly named her child Anthony, which in English means highly praiseworthy. Not to arouse suspicion as to the child's royal heritage, she called Anthony by his Greek translation which is Anthos – meaning flower.
In recent times the name Anthos became Antoniou.

My parents met and married in Maroni. A real life Romeo and Juliet story except nobody killed themselves and the marriage did not stop the feuding mothers - unlike Romeo and Juliet's deaths. Oh, and the tragedy takes place in Holloway and not in Maroni which in 1958 was twinned with the Italian town Verona.
It makes you wonder what would have happened if Romeo and Juliet had not taken their own lives. Would the marriage be a happy one or would the quarreling families drive a wedge between the star-crossed lovers. What if Romeo and Juliet could not prosper in Verona and went to far flung places to seek their fortune. Would their love endure the hardship and poverty? How would they cope with five children?
End of the day – who knows, but as old William Shakespeare wrote, "*These violent delights have violent ends*"!

The time had finally arrived. My grandmothers were expecting me. The whole village was expecting me. All three hundred of them. Maroni is a small village built on a hill, two kilometres from the sea and thirty five kilometres from Larnaca town.

Maroni was a mixed village before the intercommunal troubles of the 1960s with an average population of four hundred-seventy five percent Greek Cypriots and twenty five percent Turkish Cypriots. By the time I arrived in the late 1970s, the population stood at three hundred. Ninety nine point three percent Greek Cypriot and point seven percent English.
The twenty five percent Turkish Cypriot population moved to neighbouring villages in the south after the 1960s and then moved north after the Turkish Invasion which saw a population shift of Greek Cypriots heading south and Turkish Cypriots heading north. I don't want to go deep into Cypriot politics here. Many books have been written on the subject and many United Nation talks have taken place to reunify the island. The way I see it – if Kofi Annan, former Secretary-General of the United Nations and co-recipient of the 2001 Nobel Peace Prize couldn't settle the Cyprus issue – nobody can!

Point seven percent of the Maroni Greek Cypriot population (my two grandmothers) were informed that I would be arriving that week. They then went and informed the remaining ninety eight point six percent of the Maroni Greek

Cypriot population. Had the grandmothers spoken English, the last point seven percent would have been informed too.

I arrived at the entrance to the village by van. My aunt was in thc passenger seat and my uncle in the driver's seat. The van belonged to my uncle's father who loaned his son the van because the thirty year old Mercedes was in the garage. I was laid out in the back of the van. My mode of transport for the duration of my holiday.
My aunt was looking forward to seeing her mother, my paternal grandmother and I was apprehensive about meeting both grandmothers. Apparently they were legends.
My uncle and aunt gave me a quick briefing on the grandmothers' relationship on the drive up to the village. In short – they hated each other with a vengeance. They hated each other before my parents met. They hated each other before my parents got married. Now with stories coming back to Cyprus that my parents were having marriage troubles, well that made them hate each other even more, if that was even possible.
That was the end of the briefing.
I was fascinated to learn that they not only lived in a small village where they would bump into each other daily, but they lived in old stone houses forty feet apart. How they never killed each other was a mystery to all.
The plan was to spend a few days in the village.
My aunt said that it would be best if I initially stayed with my maternal grandmother, as my aunt and uncle would be staying with her mother. When my maternal grandmother had her fill

of me, I could join my aunt and uncle at my paternal grandmother's.
I was reassured that we would be practically next door to each other, so we would still be seeing each other and taking trips around the village and to the beach.

To be honest, I wasn't that bothered where I stayed. I wasn't worried about meeting two complete strangers.
I'd never had grandparents before.
When I was younger, (younger than I was when I arrived in Cyprus for the first time) I heard kids at school saying how good it was to visit their grandparents and how they were spoilt rotten by them. Or they stayed with their grandparents while their parents went away or they stayed with them during half term – a half term holiday.
For the first sixteen years of my life, I never left Holloway – not even for one day. So yeah, bring it on.

<*We've arrived at Maroni.*> My uncle calls out to me sitting in the back.
I sit up carefully, not to hit my head onto the roof of the van, and lean on the two front seats looking out through the widescreen.
Maroni is green. The Cyprus I saw thus far was brown.
We drove through narrow roads with small stone houses on either side. The place was deserted.
<*Where is everybody?*> I ask.
<*It's mid-afternoon.*> My uncle says. <*They are either in town, or working in the fields if they are crazy, or having an afternoon nap.*>

<*What else do they do around here?*> I enquire.
Before my uncle could answer, he applies the breaks and stops the van. Up ahead is the village square. But we can't get there because in the middle of the narrow road, there's a couple of old men sitting on chairs, leaning forward playing backgammon on a foldaway table. Adjacent to the two in the middle of the road, sit a further three old men against a café's external wall. One is fiddling with worry-beads, the other has nodded off and the third is drinking Greek coffee.
Before you ask how I know it's Greek coffee – it is the tiny cup he is holding. Greeks don't drink anything else in a cup that small. Besides, I could recognise the small Greek coffee cups a mile off. We have dozens of them in our kitchen cupboard and hundreds of them in my dad's restaurant.

I don't want to brag or go off track (again), but at the age of sixteen, I was an expert Greek coffee maker. There is an art to making Greek coffee which some people could never master.
I became proficient at it. I have made thousands during my time spent in the restaurant. I even made a Greek coffee for the former leader of the Labour Party, the late Michael Foot, when he visited my dad's restaurant. Lucky for him, my dad relaxed the dress code for the day, otherwise he would never had got in (a topical political joke of the time)!
Mr. Foot liked his Greek coffee – Metrios (medium sweet, one sugar). My dad liked his – Sketos (bitter, unsweetened) and I drank it Glykos (sweet, two sugars).

The dos and don'ts of Greek coffee.

1. You can only make it in a small copper pot with a long handle called a Briki (which sounds Turkish, but let us not go there)! Greek coffee (like Greek delights) should not be confused with the Turkish substitute, which allegedly is by far inferior in taste).
2. You cannot stir a Greek coffee. Unless you want to be called a Garathos (a donkey).
3. If you serve a Greek coffee without the Kaimaki (coffee foam) you are a Garathos.
4. Always serve Greek coffee with a glass of water. Or if the recipient is peckish, you can serve a Greek coffee with a Kolouri (Sesame covered Greek breadstick).
5. Never drink the ground coffee at the bottom of the cup.
6. If there is an old Cypriot lady nearby dressed in black with a silver cross around her neck, drink your Greek coffee (remembering to leave the sediment at the bottom). Then quickly turn the cup upside down on its saucer. Turn the cup clockwise for three full rotations and leave to settle for five minutes. After five minutes, hand the cup to the old Cypriot lady, along with five Cypriot pounds (now Euros) and she will read your fortune. If you drink all the ground coffee at the bottom of the cup, she will say *<I can see that you will meet another donkey in the near future!>*

The British national animal is the lion.
The United States has the bald eagle.
The word Garatho (donkey) is in the top ten Cypriot words used in daily conversation. As such, the donkey is now the

second national animal of Cyprus, the first being Cypriot mouflon.
I am quite certain that no other autobiography is as informative and as educational as mine.

My uncle toots the car horn.
Two of the old boys sitting against the wall look towards the car. The one sleeping stirs. The two in the middle of the road pay no attention and one slams Backgammon Checkers on the board.

Now you're going to say that I am taking the piss by deviating off the story to explain Backgammon. You are thinking that I am trying to fluff up what would be a thin paperback book.
Let me reassure you dear reader. "Fluffing up" my book has not crossed my mind since chapter three.
(By the way, if you have purchased a paperback version – thank you. A small percentage of the small royalties from the paperback sales will go to a Cypriot donkey sanctuary for sexually abused donkeys).
I was worried at first at the lack of material at the time. But I found during the course of writing my autobiography (and narrative history), that I would wake up in the middle of the night with memories I thought long forgotten. Some days I had trouble sleeping, as certain events came back to me. Some happy, some not so happy. There were the odd days that I thought I was going mad. Anyway, more on that in the Epilogue.

Cypriot culture is as important to me as is my Cockney culture. Backgammon is more important to old Cypriot men of that generation then having a mistress or two.
Cypriots have been playing "Tavli" (Backgammon) for centuries. "We" played and won at Tavli against all of "our" conquerors throughout "our" history.
"We" beat the Hellenics, the Romans, the Venetians, the Ottomans and the British.
Richard the Lionheart struggled with the game and when he wasn't invited to play at the local cafés, he used the black and white checkers to play draughts instead.
The old Cypriot men play it at lightening speeds. They can perform thousands of calculations per second whilst drinking Greek coffees one after the other. This leads to a healthy brain - perhaps a contributing factor to their longevity – which may explain why my father's generation who emigrated from Cyprus, on average, didn't live past sixty five years of age!
Arguments have been settled by Tavli. Old scores and old love rivals could be put aside during a game of Tavli. After a game the loser would kick off again, but at least peace was achieved during the game.
Once a game starts, you cannot interrupt the players for love or money.

My uncle toots the horn again....
The man with the worry beads looks towards the van and gestures the Greek recognised hand motion of "What do you want?"

This is where I pause yet again. This time, to describe a Greek Cypriot hand gesture.
Here is the Greek Cypriot hand signal for "What do you want?" – Hold your right hand out in front of you like you are going to shake somebody's hand. Slightly bend in the ring and small finger and snap your wrist, turning it one hundred and eighty degrees clockwise. "What do you want?"
Another classic Greek Cypriot hand gesture is the "Na!"
The physical hand signal is very similar to the new modern hand gesture of "talk to the hand", but the context differs.
Like "talk to the hand", you hold out your hand with palm facing your target. You then spread fingers wide and thrust your palm forward simultaneously saying "NA!", which supplements the hand gesture.
You would use "Na!" when somebody says something idiotic or acts in a stupid way.
You could also say "Na sta matia sou!" meaning "in your eyes", if somebody did something ultra-stupid.
To accompany the "Na in your eyes", you slap the back of the hand held out with your other hand.
There are hundreds of Greek Cypriot hand signals. Alas, I can't go through them all here, so I'll save them for the prequel "The Cyprus Years" out twelve months after "The Holloway Years" release date.

My uncle toots the car horn for a third (and final) time (I promise).
The old men sitting in the middle of the road reluctantly look up from their game towards us.

<*They're not going to budge,*> I say.
My uncle leans out of the open window, just about to say something, when all three of us in the car hear a screeching voice.
The old codgers sit upright and look in the opposite direction of the van.
There is something in the perspective.
I learnt about perspective in art classes.
I am looking at a painting of two old men on either end of the canvas. In the middle is the fold up table and on top of the table is the Backgammon board.
Above the Backgammon board and dead-centre of the painting, is a small black dot. The size of the dot determines the distance. This dot becomes a tiny figure, from which the perspective is perceived as being distant. However, this figure is making one hell of a racket for being so far away.
The figure is of a tiny old woman. The noise she is making gets louder and louder, but she still remains black and small and still in the centre of this Cypriot masterpiece.
My aunt is excited. I can tell from her voice when she says, <*It's my mum, your grandmother.*>
The painting is now distorted and the perspective is all wrong. The old lady has reached the Backgammon board, but still the figure is black and small.
"*Once a game starts, you cannot interrupt the players for love or money*".
Correction –you cannot interrupt the players unless you are a tiny ninja dressed in black, wearing a black headscarf and an apron dusted with flour, waving a wooden walking stick.

Did "you" really *beat the Hellenics, the Romans, the Venetians, the Ottomans and the British?*
The old woman is shouting in Greek. She lifts her apron and then her leg and simulates kicking the fold up table legs, which rouses the old Backgammon gentlemen into action. One picks up the table horizontally keeping the board steady and the other old man takes the two wooden chairs and moves to the side of the road.
My aunt gets out first and rushes to her mother. My uncle gets out next and comes to the back of the van. He opens both rear doors to let me out. I crawl out legs first, stand up and have a good ole stretch. I walk around the van and approach my aunt and the tiny deadly ninja.
<*Hello yiayia.*> I said...

* * *

Yiayia verse Yiayia...

Pappou is the Greek word for grandfather.
Yiayia is the Greek word for grandmother.
If you Google-Image the word "yiayia" the result will be hundreds of pictures of old Greek women that look like only a madman would want to mess with them.
Just have a look at this book's cover. Top left picture is of an ugly teenage Pan with paternal yiayia on the left (as you look at the picture) and maternal yiayia on the right. Paternal yiayia is dressed in black and has been wearing black since my

paternal pappou passed away when my father was twelve. My maternal yiayia is not dressed in black.

I spent four days in the village of Maroni. I was sixteen years old when I met my grandmothers for the first time and I was sixteen years of age when I saw them for the last time.
For many reasons, it took twenty years for me to go back to Cyprus and twenty three years to return to the village of Maroni - that would be for my father's funeral.
There are a lot of "what ifs" in my life. One of those is not, <*What if I never met the grandmothers.*>
However brief the visit was, it has given me some fond memories of them both, as well as some unanswered questions.

Conversations in this subchapter were spoken in Greek and kindly translated for your convenience.

<*Hello yiayia,*> I said. <*I'm Panico – Antonis's son,*> I thought I'd had to clarify since I was grandchild number twenty-odd.
<*I know who you are, I've been expecting you.*> she says as she reaches up and pulls at my cheeks.
<*When I heard the car, I knew it was you.*> She says to me.
She turns to her daughter and grabs her arm. Then points at the two old men with the Backgammon set and shouts to them, <*Did you two idiots try to stop my grandson coming into the village?*> She then encircles my arm and she leads us out of the town square towards her house.

My uncle gets back in the van and tells us he will meet us at the house once he finds a place to park the van in this small village on a hill with narrow roads.
We walk down a narrow road, yayia in the middle with my aunt and myself on either side.
We pass by small stone houses with front doors wide open. Outside these houses, sitting on chairs or on the front steps, are women of varying ages. Some are crocheting with white lace, others are peeling or cutting vegetables into a bowl.
My yiayia drags us along, pausing only to proudly announce <*This is my grandson – from England.*>
We turn a corner and up ahead there is another old woman. This one is running and then when she spots us she slows and then hobbles towards us. She approaches and my aunt says to me, <T*his is your other yiayia – your mother's mum.*>
Yiayia number two (my mum's mum) holds her arms out wide, readying an embrace and calls out, <I*s this my Panagioti*?>

Early on in the book, I stated that my name is Panico. I didn't lie, but the truth is that I was Christened Panagiotis.
Panico is the Cypriot derivative of the Greek Panagiotis.
Stay with me now.....
Panagiotis (masculine) is from Panagia (feminine) - the Greek title given to The Virgin Mary, the mother of Jesus Christ.
Panagia translates to the All-Holy or All-Saints.
Pan– the Greek (and English) word for "all" and Agia (or Agios) for "holy", or "Saint".

Nobody has ever called me Panagiotis. Shit, Panico was hard enough to grow up with in Holloway. Imagine what state I'd be in if I was enrolled in school as a Panagiotis?
Don't take me the wrong way. If you are a Panagiotis and you just happen to be reading this – don't take offence man!
You're probably twice as handsome as I, and were raised to be confident and had holidays and were held high on a pedestal as are all Greek sons. I bet your parents bought you a BMW when you turned seventeen......and.
Sorry –I nearly lost it there.

<*Panagioti-mou.*> "mou" meaning "my".
<*Go to your* (other) *yiayia.*> My aunt tells me.
Easier said than done. The yiayia with her arm wrapped around mine has put me in a Ju-JitSu arm-lock.

I wasn't going to be called Panico/Panagioti.
Apparently when I was born, I was named something totally different. I was given a name from my dad's side of the family. Then a message was sent to my mother from her mother.
My maternal grandmother had health issues and she went to church to pray for her ailment to be cured. She promised in church, that if her illness passed and she recovered, she would not only light a weekly candle, but would arrange for a grandchild to be called after the Virgin Mary – Panagia.
I was Christened Panagiotis and my yiayia was healed.
My mother told me the story after I came home from school in tears after a heavy day of Pani-blossom name calling.

<Is that supposed to make me feel better? A lifetime of piss-takes so that my grandmother can dance the Zeimbekiko?> I asked.

Here I am, a decade later and the yiayia I cured with my sacrifices is embracing me and calling me Panagiotis so that it winds up my other yiayia.
Yep, I suppose it was worth it. I feel a connection to these two old ladies. I feel loved. I notice the strength in them. I suspect, they will kill for their family. They are proper Greek Cypriot yiayias!

My arms are being pulled from their sockets. They are pulling me in opposite directions and I don't know in which direction to head in. I am standing in the road equal distance from both of my grandmothers' houses.
Paternal yiayia doesn't acknowledge maternal yiayia and continues to hold onto me pulling me towards the right.
<I've made some cake.> she says.
Maternal yiayia also ignores her "sin-pethera" (Greek word for family in-law) and pulls me to the left and she says, *<let me show you where your mum grew up.>*
They still refuse to utter a single word to each other, but I can see their eyes squinting just like Clint Eastwood's in The Good, The Bad and The Ugly, just before he shoots dead a dozen hombres.
<I've made Mahallebi,> maternal yiayia says, *<your mother's favourite.>*
Mahallebi is a refreshing Cypriot pudding/sweet served ice cold with rosewater or rose-syrup and ice cold water.

It is clear that the name "Mahallebi" is not Greek Cypriot. It's most likely Turkish and introduced to the Turkish Cypriots first. Best not mention it to the yiayias.
It's hot and I could do with some Mehallebi. I'll even settle for the ice cold water. I start to slightly veer towards the left.
Not to be outdone, paternal yiayia goes for the bullseye. *<I've made Kalo-Prama.>* literal translation is "good-thing"... Good-Thing Cake. A Semolina cake with syrup drizzle.
Nothing Turkish about Good-Thing Cake. Nobody and I mean nobody born to a Greek Cypriot parent or parents could refuse Good-Thing.
I level up and turn towards the right, still in the vice-like grip of both ladies. I see sadness in the eyes of maternal yiayia. I stop in the middle of the road. I'm in a dilemma. I'm going to hurt one of these old ladies. I need time to think.
<Can I have a photo with me and the yiayias,> I say and hand my camera to my aunt.
Both yiayias freeze on the spot and their grip loosens. They are both ready leg-it. They are preparing to protest, but which one is to disappoint me by refusing first? They look at each other, begging the other to make the first move and decline their grandson's request. A grandson who came all the way from London to see them especially.
Time seems to stand still. Neither is prepared to decline the request, but not one of them is happy with the idea.
The stalemate is broken by my aunt who scolds both women and snaps, *<Will you two do as your grandson asks. We had a long drive up, we are hot and hungry and thirsty.>*

We line up against a stone wall with me in the middle keeping the old biddies apart. My aunt takes the photo.
Back in England, nobody could believe that I managed to capture the two old ladies together in a photo. This is the one and only photo that exists with them in the same frame.
I've never seen my parents' wedding photos. In fact, I don't know of any in existence, but if there were any, these old ladies wouldn't be in them.

A brief moment of silence is broken by my paternal yiayia. She pulls at my arm and says, <*Now you and my daughter will come to my house to freshen up and eat.*> Totally ignoring the other yiayia.
My maternal yiayia retorts, <*No, you will come back to my house.*> She pulls at my other arm whilst ignoring the other yiayia and my aunt.
I'm stuck in the middle. I am being tugged at and now voices are being raised, insistent that I follow one of them.
I look at my aunt with pleading eyes and she comes through.
With a stern tone my aunt says, <*Mum, I am coming home with you so we can catch up with the gossip and your grandson is going with his other yiayia. He will join us later.*> With that, my aunt drags paternal yiayia off.
<*Let's go yiayia,*> I say to maternal yiayia. <*I'm craving Mahallebi!*>

The remainder of that day was spent toing and froing between the yiayias houses. I was feeling the stress of being emotionally blackmailed. I didn't want to upset either yiayia. I had a late heavy lunch with one and then a heavier dinner with the other. I ate three types of desserts, drank endless fizzy drinks and forced down ten kilograms of watermelon with a kilo of halloumi. Halloumi is a perfect accompaniment with watermelon by the way.

The sun was setting and a decision had to be made- where I was to sleep for the duration of my stay in the village. Both yiayias were waiting for an answer as I bounced between the two stone houses.

My aunt came up trumps again. She convinced her mum that since she was to have my aunt and uncle staying over, it was only fair that I kept the other yiayia company. Sorted!

I went and told maternal yiayia that I was staying over.

She showed me to my bedroom and lit the mosquito repellent candle.

<*Where is the toilet?*> I asked ready to burst.

<*Let me show you, follow me.*>

I follow and she leads me to the small back yard. She picks up a torch from a shelf fixed to the outside wall, switches it on and points to a small wooden shed. An outhouse.

<*The toilet's in there,*> she says.

I walk towards the outhouse, open the door and,<*WHAT THE FUCK!!!!*>

* * *

The World Record for holding your poo in...

--warning, this subchapter is crap!

I am disappointed to say that my research on the subject is lacking. During my preparation for this chapter, I googled "holding in your poo" with safe search switched off and received a warning from my broadband service provider for accessing inappropriate material. Not only that, today, all the adverts that pop-up on web pages are for baby nappies, incontinence pads and local prostitutes that offer to crap on you for your pleasure. I have had to install an additional pop-up blocker and adware remover as well as cleaning my cache daily.

I did find information on constipation which isn't really relevant because I did not have constipation.

By the way, the world record for the longest constipation case is one hundred and two days. There was also a web page on a Chinese man who was constipated on and off for twenty-two years and he had to have surgery to remove eleven kilograms of poo. Again not relevant to my story but quite informative.

I accidently hit on a website called "ratemypoo.com".

I mean, what kind of sick individuals upload pictures of their floating turds in a toilet-pan (oh, another nickname) for other sick individuals to rate them out of ten?

So I changed my search parameters to "voluntarily holding in your poo". There were links to chat rooms and forums and the

general consensus was – why the hell would you want to hold your poo in?
So I have to conclude by stating that there is no world record for holding in one's poo when one is desperate to unload.
So from this day onwards, I have to acknowledge that I may be the unofficial record holder for holding in one's poo whilst bursting at the seams. I will write to The Guinness Book of World Records for recognition and will forward this chapter as an affidavit.

The unofficial record is four days. The four whole days I spent in the village of Maroni.
The unintended attempt to break the record started on my first night in the village.

I slam the door to the outhouse shut. This is my second attempt to enter the outhouse. My grandmother handed me the torch and went back inside the house ten minutes ago and here I am, still standing outside the shithouse, trying to build up enough courage to re-enter.
I am bursting to go number ones and number twos. I could go for a number one anywhere in this small yard, but I need to have a poo. I need to take a dump, see a man about a horse, release the chocolate hostage, drop a load, take a dump, shit a brick, launch a torpedo, lighten the load, make a mud pie, lay a chocolate egg ...... and in Greek "na sheso!"
I take a deep breath and hold it. With torch light beaming towards the front, I open the door for the third and final time.

Once again, the smell hits me like a Cypriot donkey kicking me in the face. I hear flies buzzing. I hear mosquitos screaming *<let us out.>* My eyes water, but this time I enter as the door closes behind me on a spring.
I shine the torch into the dark outhouse and there is the chair I got a glimpse of on attempt number two (pun). It is an old wooden chair with a wicker back. The seat is missing. Under the chair, directly below the missing seat, is a hole. A six inch diameter borehole to hell. It is obvious to me that my grandmother is having aiming difficulties – enough said!
I shine the torch down the hole. It is deep with layers reminiscent to a painting depicting Dante's inferno – a journey to hell.
The light emanating from the torch is consumed by the hole's darkness. It might be my imagination but, haunted cries can be heard coming deep within the pit.

I read in a horror magazine that a "hole to hell" was discovered in Russia.
During a scientific experiment, a Russian scientist called Aleksei drilled a borehole so deep, that it broke through into a void which consumed laser beams when aimed into the hole.
When Aleksei and his team lowered a microphone into the borehole, tortured screams were heard.
The hole in my yiayia's outhouse may well be the second of such a hole to be discovered.
I was thinking of writing to these scientists and informing them that I discovered another A-hole - in Cyprus!
(*Groan*)

It's time to make a decision. To fish or cut bait. Or a more appropriate expression - to shit or get off the pot.
I can no longer keep hold of the lungful of air and have to exhale. On exhaling, I have no choice but to inhale a lifetime of stinks. My nose burns and my throat constricts.
I turn around to face the door and loosen the cord around my shorts. I pull my shorts and pants down to my knees and with quivering legs, I begin a slow squat. The chair must be lower than I thought. Either that, or my legs are refusing to bend as it takes an eternity for my bum cheeks to make contact with the chair's seat-less frame. Finally, my arse makes contact. Then something sharp scratches my left arse cheek. Thinking I've been bitten, I pan-ic and shoot up straight whilst pants and shorts make a slow slide to my ankles.
<*Please don't touch the floor.*> I beg my shorts.
I can't do it. I keep thinking that a fly will shoot up my bum-hole. I've have to abandon dam–busting for now. I will make another attempt in the morning. Before the old lady wakes up. Buts that's half the problem. I can't hold my pee in for a second longer. I'm desperate for Jimmy (Jimmy Riddle – Piddle).
So with garments around my ankles, I shuffle turn around to face the hole. Then I'm confronted with another predicament. How the hell do I piss in a six inch hole with a chair in the way? How the hell does yiayia manage it? Oh yeah...sorry!
I shuffle backwards until my arse touches the door. I take hold of my willy (I was a late developer) in hand and aim under the chair at an angle. Urinc gushcs out hitting the back edge of the hole. I change the angle and some urine goes into the hole and

a good percentage splashes on the chair legs. But I'm on a high. I don't give a shit. And for four days – I didn't!

* * *

Tavli II (Backgammon)

On the last day in the village – with my guts ready to explode, I found myself alone and bored in the village with my maternal yiayia. My aunt and uncle had errands to run with paternal yiayia, so I decided to go for a stroll around the village and planned to end up in the café later for a coke.

I set off. No map, no compass and no clue where I was going, but that's me...adventurous!

Ten minutes later I stopped. I'm stood on the outskirts of the village. I would like to describe to you the wonderful scenery and the flora and fields with watermelons, the blue sky and the people I met on my journey...

But it was too hot. I was thirsty. I didn't see a soul and sweat was running down my head and into my eyes. What a stupid idea this was. I turned around and walked back, heading for the café where I should have aimed for in the first place.

What did you expect? I was sixteen. I wasn't a rambler!

I got to the café. There were the same old boys (I think they were the same– old men do look alike) sitting outside the café. This time four of them were playing Tavli (Backgammon for those who missed it the first time) and the other old geezer is fiddling with his Vraka.

Vraka is the traditional Cypriot trousers or pantaloons. Short to the knees and very baggy around the arse and crotch. A must wear for old Cypriot men during the hot summer months where one can allow his sagging ball bag to swing and cool the bag's contents without hindrance.
I doubt very much if any old men wear them today,

There is an old Cypriot song called "Tin Gerimin Tin Vraka" (very roughly translated – the fucking Vraka).
Every Cypriot parent around in the sixties and seventies would teach their kids the lyrics. At weddings or social gatherings, the parents would drag their kids out and put them in the middle of the throng where they would then proceed to sing "Tin Vraka" in a high pitch screech whilst the little shits' parents would look in admiration.
Yes, I know the words, but I swear I never sang it in public.
Come to think of it, there was another song our parents would force us to memorise and sing to visiting relatives and that song was the dreaded (translated) "Maria in the Yellow Dress".
Any Cypriots my age reading this would probably come out in a cold sweat at its mention.
The song is about Maria and her adulterous relationship with a neighbour!
Oh shit – I've just thought of another....about a carriage pulled by two horses.
I won't continue to bore you with traditional crap....... Back to the story...

I walked past the old men and went inside where I bought a 7-Up drink and then explained whose grandson I was. The café owner knew my parents, but not well enough to have the 7-Up on the house! He knew my Yiayias very well, but the café owner played ignorant. Can't blame him really. Returning Cypriots and Charlies are rich pickings for the natives.
I thanked him regardless and walked back outside where it was no hotter or cooler than inside.

There was an empty chair next to the old man with the snazzy Vraka, so I went and sat next to him (in the shade) and we both watched the other four men playing the two games of Tavli.
The old gentlemen played in complete silence – no doubt enemies putting their differences aside for the game.
The speed at which they played was mesmerising. The dice were thrown against the wooden sides of the board and no sooner than the dice settled, the players would move the checkers, slam the board and tut if cornered by the opponent.
The only sound to be heard coming from the old boys was the slurping of the Greek coffee or the rattling of the old-man-in-the-pantaloon's testicles as they hit each other like castanets with the freedom they had to roam, every time the old boy shifted to a more comfortable position on the wooden chair.

The game to my right finished with one final slam of checker against wood. One of the old men stood, waved a hand gesture in the air which meant another time, and off he went.

The remaining old boy looks up from the board. He eyes the one in the baggy pants and when he notices that he has nodded off, he looks in my direction.
<*Do you play?*> He asks me in Greek.
<*Er yeah...I play.*> I reply back – in Greek.
The Greek word for "Er" is "Eh!" (Including the exclamation).
He motions a hand gesture to indicate – take the seat.
It's too hot for anymore words.

I learnt how to play Tavli at my cousin's house. His dad taught him and he showed me. Then I beat him and we haven't played since.
My dad taught me poker one Christmas. I taught my mates at school and I ate free for weeks. Then they never played poker with me again.
Now I don't want to come over as arrogant and start bragging, but I can pick up board and card games so easily that in no time I can master them like a....a master!
I learnt chess in a week and later won a class chess tournament. When I was awarded a prize of just two felt tip pens, I never played again!
I once accumulated so much money in a game of Monopoly with little brother, that in order to prolong the game and his torture, I would give him "bank bonuses" of a thousand pounds for passing go – only so that he could give me the money back when he landed on one of my many hotels. I ended up with almost all the bank's money. I even changed the rules and offered little brother "double bank bonuses" so that I

could purchase "Community Chest", "Chance" and "Free Parking". I was that good!
Little brother played me plenty of times.

I take a seat opposite my old Tavli opponent and crack my knuckles for effect.
The old boy stands slightly and cracks his knees, back and neck.
The old boy picks up a dice and throws a five. I pick up the other dice and throw a three. He starts!
The old boy picks up both dice, throws a total of eight (a five and a three) and moves his checker into position. All in under zero point three seconds.
I throw a total of eleven (a six and a five).
I pause to think what checker move would be to my advantage.
I pick one and tap it on the board counting the moves.... (tap) one, (tap) two, (tap) three. No, I change my mind. I put the checker down and pick another. I tap that checker on the board and count the moves...(tap) one, (tap) two, (tap) three, (tap) four, (tap) five, (tap) six, (I pause...tap) seven, (tap) eight, (tap) nine, (tap) ten, (tap) eleven. I place the checker down in its new slot.

The old geezer slams the board shut. Stands. Fttts at me. He makes the sound <*Fttt,*> whilst rolling his eyes and flicking his head once in an upward motion. Then the old git buggers off!

I guess I won by default then!

* * *

Goodbye Maroni – Goodbye Cyprus

I hate to say it, but the four days in the village of Maroni dragged on a bit. Not only because I was desperate to go for a dump, but also because there wasn't much to do in a small village – except to take bets on which yiayia would snap first and chin the other!

I leave the village without getting to the bottom of the story of why the yiayias are sworn enemies. I did ask each one in turn when I thought they were off-guard, but neither would even acknowledge the other.

I leave the village bloated and with greenish tinged veins under my eyes. I must be fermenting on the inside. I am also humming on the outside from the lack of bathing.

Yiayia did offer to fill up a tin bath, but I declined due to the fear of farting in the tub in my condition.

I thanked the yiayias for their generous hospitality and for the unconditional love they showed me.

I promised to return every year to visit...but maybe not to stay. It was a promise that I had every intention of keeping.

With suitcase in hand, I followed my uncle and aunt to the van which was parked on the other side of the small village.

Behind us, at a distance from each other were the old dears. As we walked down the path, a few villagers came out of their houses to bid us "kalo taksidi" (a safe journey).

We walk through the town square and I spot an old man waving at me to come over. My aunt stops up ahead, turns around and looks at me. <*It's your pappou, your mum's dad*,> she says.
I stopped. I felt stunned and confused. My mum told me that her parents divorced when she was a young girl. I knew he was alive and living somewhere in Cyprus. What I wasn't aware of was that he lived in the same village as his ex-wife. The village where I've just spent four days in.
<*Shall I go*?> I asked my aunt. I want to go, but I'd better seek some advice on this sensitive matter.
There was no shortage of widows in the village but divorces were a rarity. Nobody divorced in Cyprus in those days. They fled a marriage but never divorced.
<*He's your pappou, you should go*,> my uncle says, giving me some much needed male advice.
My pappou continues to give me the Greek hand signal for "come here". I drop my suitcase and walk over.
I approach and say <*hello*> like an idiot.
<*I heard you were in the village*,> my pappou says. <*What is your name, whose son are you*?> He asks.
<*I'm Panico, your daughter's son.*> He only has one daughter so it narrows it down a bit.
<*So you're my grandson......*> and before he could say anything else, his ex-wife, my maternal grandmother comes up to us.

I look at her with a "look who it is expression" on my face.
<*You don't want to talk to him!*> She says and pushes me away from him.
I turn around and there is my pappou, walking away.
I never saw him or any of my grandmothers again.

We arrived back at the village of Harry-dipped-in-the-poo. After I visited the toilet, they renamed the village to Pan-did-one-hell-of-a-poo!

CHAPTER 15:-PAKEMAN STREET III

There were some good times. There were some bad times. The years passed.
We boys had our own bedrooms and the girls shared.
We were all getting bigger. Our parents were still volatile.
Normal family life I guess.
I remember the last time my parents fought. It was that magical hour of four in the morning.
There is something special about that time. It is a time favoured by the police when they raid suspects' homes. The time when the body is still halfway between sleep and alertness. When you are woken up at that time, you are disorientated. It takes a while to sync in to what is happening. Then you realise that it is your parents arguing again.

Four in the morning was the average time my father would come home after closing the restaurant. Most of the time we would not hear him open the front door, light a cigarette, go to the toilet, light another cigarette and then go to bed. Other times, we might hear muffled voices coming from their bedroom. That night, I heard them shouting.
I would sit up and try and listen. I no longer covered my head under the blankets. That is partly because I never made my bed properly and half way through the night, my sheets and blankets ended up on the floor.

Some days the shouting would be brief and you could go back to sleep almost immediately. Other times, the shouts turned to cries. That night I heard something else. I heard my big brother shouting. I instantly got up and went to investigate.
I went down the attic stairs and opened my door to a bright landing. The top floor and middle floor landing lights were on. My brother's bedroom door was open and before I had the chance to look in his room, I heard him on the middle landing outside my parents' room.
My dad was six foot tall. With us boys, his bark was worse than his bite. Not to say that we never felt a smack, but coming from dad they were rare but meaningful!
Big brother was also six foot at that time, lean and wiry, with no bark or bite. A gentle dude - when he wasn't pinning me to the floor and gobbing in my face that was.
<*Enough*!!!> I heard big brother shout.
That angered my dad and he came out of the room to confront my brother.
<*Yeah enough!*> I shout as I walked down to the middle landing and stood behind my brother...just in case.
Then my big sister opens her door and she too joins in on our uprising.
Although little brother and little sister no longer bawled their eyes out during the parents' early morning fights, I knew from past experiences that they would be under the covers holding their ears with both hands and with eyes closed tight.
Big brother said something like <*You should be ashamed of yourselves*,> followed by an incoherent rant.
I shouted out <*You tell them!*>

Then big brother looked at me and told me to <*shut the fuck up!*> Dad looked confused and prepared to re-affirm his alpha-male status. Then he actually did look ashamed.

There was no power shift. It was not a show of strength on big brother's part. I acknowledged later that big brother had bottled it all up and this was the cork popping. He shouted at both parents, tears streaming with anger and frustration.
Mum came out to console him and dad went back inside his room. I took big brother's advice and never said another word. I have a habit of rubbing people up the wrong way and one wrong word could set them all off again. I went back up to the attic and left them to it.
Silence descended. I picked up the sheets and blankets off the floor and bundled them onto the bed. I crawled in and tried to sleep, wondering what the next day or days would bring.
That was the last night we kids were woken up by our parents – that I could remember. That wasn't to say that they stopped arguing though!
It would be great to say that my parents became a loving couple, but alas this was not to be.

Not sure if it was weeks or months that passed after that night of rebellion. And I am not implying that this was the reason which led to dad packing his bags and leaving home, but leave he did. Weeks later he returned with his laundry. A year later he left home again and months later he returned. That was the pattern with them until he left for good, but before that – he had a wedding to organise and pay for.

* * *

The years pass at Pakeman Street...

...to be followed by the last years at Pakeman Street.

For some reason, I cannot remember the sequence of the following events. The timeline is all wrong – I know that, but I can't for the life of me straighten it out. It's all a jigsaw that I cannot put together.
There was so much going on.
There is so much I cannot write. I have to skim over some incidents as it is not a book about my siblings' coping mechanisms but mine. Besides, I don't think it is fair on them. I wrote about events that centered on me. I am the centre of my universe after all!

Mum stopped hitting us – probably because big brother snatched her broomstick off her, took it out into the garden and karate chopped it in several pieces.
When dad left home the first time, she seemed content with the idea. Not happy but at ease, like she expected this day to happen. Likewise when he returned, she expected it and for a short period of time, they were civil to each other.

I left school. I got an apprenticeship as a Television Engineer. I did well in electronics at school and I had a knack of repairing appliances which we kids broke.

I told my dad that I couldn't work full-time in the restaurant. I did not want that lifestyle, but to appease him and to earn some extra cash, I worked there on the weekends. I had a Ford Capri to run. Airwolf!

Big brother worked in various dress factories as a cutter. He left home and rented a one bedroom bedsit. I went round to visit him and we heated tinned hotdogs in the kettle. Obviously, we took them out of the tin first.
Like dad, he returned home, then left again and then returned.

Little sis was doing well in school. The situation at home was difficult and this took its toll.

Little brother was smashing up the house.
We all had family counselling. We were all out of our depth with this. That pit in my stomach from the days of Mayton Street and the early years of Pakeman Street returned.

Big sis got engaged. Then she married and left home.
There was a period of domestic normality leading up to the wedding. My parents' relationship with each other and with their children was calm and respectful. They were a partnership.
We were included in the buildup and on the big day itself-
We were a family.
The wedding was huge. One thousand guests pinning money on the bride and groom. I wore a suit for the first time. My mother danced and my father saw to all the rich people.

As you can see, I have no stupid exploits to mention. No dog-shit or childish pranks.
Every book has the odd boring chapter and chapter fifteen is this book's non-event.

* * *

The last years at Pakeman Street.

To be followed by the last days at Pakeman Street...

Dad left home for good. He stayed in one of the flats above the restaurant. He moved a woman in and I stopped going to the restaurant out of loyalty for my mother. I hardly saw him.
My mother was a different woman. We became close and I felt that she depended on me – not financially, as my dad still paid the bills and gave mum money every week, although he could have given more. No, mum depended on me for sanity I guess.
I was a qualified television engineer on shit money. I wasn't a loner but I wasn't out every weekend either. I had a small group of friends from school and we met up a few times a month. We did the odd pub crawl and went away once to the Algarve for a lads' holiday, except the only lads' stuff we did was to get pissed most nights. I still had that element of harmless craziness about me, but that was eroding away with every day that past.
Psycho-Pan was turning into a moody git.
I elected to stay home more than a young man should. I often made excuses not to go out. I started to enjoy my own company

and often sat on my bed in the attic watching videos and smoking the odd joint. I recorded and watched so many episodes of "The Phil Silvers Show" that I became an authority on Sgt Bilko.

If I wasn't in the attic, then I would be in big brother's room. He was back home after a spell living with a girlfriend. Big brother was into Pink Floyd. We would smoke a joint and listen to The Floyd. We would also listen to little brother kicking in his bedroom door or punching a wall. We were all at a loss with his behaviour. The counselling was ongoing and we were impatient with the results.

Enough said on this matter!

Getting stoned seemed like a solution.

It was an answer to my boredom and an answer to the situation at home.

One night, something strange happened. Something triggered what today is known as obsessive behaviour.

At that time it was known as going crazy!

I don't think there was one specific action. Probably an accumulation of past and current events. Truth is, I don't know, but today I can hazard a guess. Later on throughout my life I've had certain episodes, but nothing like the first night it happened.

I was the last one up when the rest of the family had gone to bed. I locked the front door and made my way up to my room. Suddenly, I stopped halfway up the first set of stairs. I had a feeling that the gas cooker was on. So I went back down to the kitchen and made sure all the gas hobs were turned off. As I went to go back upstairs, thoughts of the house burning down entered my head. I couldn't be certain that I checked all four gas hob controls, so I went back down and stood by the cooker. One by one, I turned on the gas rings and then turned them off again.

I then had an urge to check the back door. It was locked. I unlocked it then locked it to be certain.

I walked back up the stairs and this time I made it to the first floor landing before I stopped. My head was itching like mad and no amount of scratching could ease that feeling. It eased as I walked back down and on my way to the kitchen, I checked the front door.

I walked into the kitchen and sat on a chair by the kitchen table where I placed my head in my hands. After ten minutes, I lifted my head up and stared hard at the cooker. I focused on the controls. They were all turned up – to the off position. I counted them. One – off. Two – off. Three – off. Four – off. Then the grill – off. Oven – off. I got up and walked out of the kitchen and headed towards my bedroom.

This time I never even made it to the stairs.

During the last years of Pakeman, I learnt to cope with my odd behaviour. I never told a soul and never made it obvious that I would check and double check the cooker, or the plugs in the electrical sockets, or both doors, front and back. I found that if I gave the kitchen cooker a once over whilst humming a different tune per occasion, I would not need to re-visit. So I would check doors with one tune and the cooker with another. Yep – sounds crazy huh!

Eventually, I would be the last up to bed every night. And some nights were very long.
Some days I would arrive to work half asleep.

I loved my job. I was on low wages, but I didn't care.
For somebody who spent most evenings at home, I couldn't wait for the morning when I could go to work.
I loved being in the workshop. I loved the challenge of repairing a faulty electrical appliance. For an alleged introvert, I loved carrying my toolbox into a customer's house and repairing their television set. I always refused a cup of tea though.
I loved the people I worked for and with.
My boss and his wife were Greek. Slightly younger than my parents' age. Their relationship opened my eyes to an alternative loving lifestyle that one could have with the right partner.
Then there was Christos - the senior engineer and later, the best man at my wedding. My eldest daughter's Godfather. My adoptive older brother who had tolerance to teach me everything there was about repairing televisions and videos.
I worked under his supervision for eight years including the four I served as an apprentice and not once did he lose patience with me.
We kept in-touch on and off for twenty five years, then lost contact totally. I regretted the times I said I would get back in touch, then put it off for another week.
Then two years ago, I received the deeply upsetting news that he passed away.

* * *

The last days at Pakeman Street.

I became bored with smoking marijuana. I wasn't getting that buzz I once got. The more I smoked, the more lethargic and depressed I got. There had to be something more. I was hoping my life would change. I was only twenty two, but felt that my life wasn't going anywhere. As a kid I was so full of life. I was full of mischief. Sadly, that Pan was gone (down-the-Pan)!

I had some business cards printed.
P.A Electronics
T.V & Video Engineer
I had a few calls and it got me out of the house some evenings. It also gave me a chance to earn some extra money which I needed as Airwolf (my Ford Capri) needed new brakes and a new exhaust. I considered maybe going to see my dad and working part time in the restaurant, but it was getting on to a couple of years since I'd seen him and I couldn't build up the courage to go and see him. Also, I thought that would upset my mother, so I put that idea out of my mind.
Then on one evening whilst out doing a private repair, I found something that I'd been waiting for. I found something that changed my life forever.

I remember a discussion I had with my big brother and one of his mates during another sitting of listening to "Wish You Were Here" whilst brain dead. I remember it was my last night smoking dope. I remember that I couldn't have said what I said had I not been high.

<*I've met a girl.*> I started.
<*She's my barber's daughter. She works with him in the salon and when I go and have my haircut, I would hear this loud Cockney Greek Cypriot girl chatting with her clients and laughing. She is unbelievably beautiful and has these deep dimples in her cheeks noticeable from a mile off, even when she is not smiling – which is hardly ever.*>

My brother mimes the wanking sign, but I continue.

<*I never spoke to her in the shop. What would be the point? She's well out of my league. Besides, she is not my taste. I like moody, depressingly ugly girls that I may have a chance with!*
She probably thinks I'm weird anyway, as I keep staring at her through the mirror while I am having a haircut.
My barber remembered I handed him one of my business cards and he asked me to go round to his house as his video player was broken. From the moment she opened the door we got chatting. She introduced me to her mother. Her father, my barber, was at The Arsenal match. She showed me the broken video and the fault.
From the first minute, I knew what the problem was. It wasn't the video. It was the dodgy pirate video copy of Rambo–First Blood II. But I wasn't going to let on. I opened the video player and pretended to adjust the tape guides. Then we chatted some more. It turns out we have nothing in common except Arsenal, but we talked to each

other like we've known each other for years. Then it occurs to me that it could be the hairdresser in her that chats so freely.
I spent over an hour in the house and when I finally ran out of things to adjust, I admitted that it was not the video player that's at fault and proved this by recording something off the T.V and playing it back.
As I left her house, I realised that I had forgotten to charge my standard call-out rate of five pounds.
These past weeks, I went back for three haircuts. I waited for her dad to nip out to the bookies and whilst he was gone, I asked her out.>

<*Don't tell me – she said yes?*> Big Brother's mate asks.
<*Is she blind?*> big brother says.
<*Yes and no,*> I reply.
Big brother turns to his mate and laughs. <*You wait and see,*> he tells his mate. <*This idiot will go and get married, cause it's just the thing this idiot would do.*>

* * *

Leaving Pakeman Street.

Sixteen months after that conversation with big brother and his mate, I left Holloway for good.
Hankies out ladies.....
It was love at fifth (or sixth) sight. Or love at first conversation. I married my barber's daughter. I married the girl that brought the young crazy Pan back. I married the girl who tells me often that she saved my life. I married the girl whose family still

owes me five pounds for the call-out charge to repair their video.
I was told (by some) that I was rushing into marrying "My Annie" as she was my first real girlfriend. Which is partly true. The real girlfriend that is.
I did have a couple of girlfriends. Nothing too serious. One girl I even brought home for my mother's perusal, but mum hated her for two reasons. One reason was that when my mum asked her what she would like to drink, this girl said <*Whiskey*!>
The other reason was that mum found out through the grapevine that this girl's grandmother was hanged in Holloway Women's Prison. No it wasn't Ruth Ellis.

Luckily for me, "My Annie's" family have yet to murder anybody. Awkwardly for me, "My Annie" has the same first name (and now surname) as my mother.
Don't go all Sigmund on me. It was pure coincidence. Ninety three percent of Greek Cypriot girls are called Androulla.
Shit, I've now gone and mentioned her real name, which she hates. She hates "My Annie" too.

Greek Cypriots have masculine and feminine versions of all known names. For example...
Andrew – Andrew-la (spelt Androulla).
Tassos – Tasso-ula.
Harry – Harry-ola (spelt Harroulla).
You get my drift.

Anyway – back to leaving Pakeman Street.

I left.
The Holloway years ended.

.

.

.

.

.

.

.

It is an anticlimactic way of finishing ones autobiography – Sorry!

.

.

.

.

.

.

.

I feel like I have to add something......

CHAPTER 16:-HAD TO BE THERE MOMENTS AND MISCELLANEOUS TALES

We (you guys and I) have almost reached the end of my autobiography. Thank you for sticking around.
Whilst writing this illiteracy masterpiece, I was racking my brains desperately trying to rekindle (excuse the pun – it is by no means a subconscious effort to get you to score me high on Kindle reviews – to be honest, as long as my kids enjoyed it and can excuse my oddities, that's all that matters.......however it would be a kick in the balls for any negative comments, especially as I've spilled my sorry emotional guts out) any long lost memories to add to the book. It was only after I would finish one chapter that something would come back - a forgotten memory which now would not fit in said completed chapter – not unless I undertook a complete chapter re-write. So the answer was to leave random memories out or include them here.
Guess what the outcome was?

* * *

Carol

I was a mid-teen and working at my dad's new restaurant after school. It was the Christmas party season and the restaurant

was fully booked out on a weekday for a civil servant's private X-mas office party.
Almost eighty tanked up females and ten males were seated (civil servants – the second worse profession for getting pissed, the first being law enforcement) and all letting loose, looking to pull any of the waiters and kitchen staff. Even Hadji, our Turkish dish-washer-uppa, who walked with a limp wasn't safe and that was from one of the male civil servants – most likely a senior manager!
My dad was giving them the full Greek Cypriot experience including dressing up one of the waiters in a traditional Cypriot Vraka who then proceeded to perform Greek dancing with tables in his mouth. He then smashed plates on his head and waved a large Cypriot tray with a bottle of wine and filled glasses at its centre (please Google/Youtube Cypriot Vraka to get the full appreciation, otherwise, a full description of Vraka dancing would need a chapter of its own).
Whilst some would say, the party was a success, you have to remember this was a Christmas party and not Zorba's bachelor party!
One of the ladies came up to my dad a bit flustered and asks in a demanding tone that only women can–
<Tony, can we have carols please...>
(I think I mentioned it before, if not here goes. Tony was my dad's English name derived from Antoniou – Greek for Anthony).
My dad has that concerned look on his face. He lifts one eyebrow up like Roger Moore and says in a thick Greek accent......... *<Carol? Who's Carol?>*

I cracked up.
My dad asked one of the female waitresses (who was perfectly safe) to go in the female toilets and check if Carol was in there and that she was ok...
I cracked up again......
I told you it was a had-to-be-there moment!

* * *

How do you make gunpowder?

It's very simple, I told my younger brother. Stick with me kid and you'll learn a lot!
The idea seemed plausible.
We get as many matchsticks as possible, cut the ends off (the explosive end), grind them down, place them in a cardboard toilet-roll holder and then tape one end shut. The other end we seal tightly up - but for a bit of rag soaked in dad's Zivania sticking out.
Behold, a homemade stick of dynamite.
What could possibly go wrong?

Zivania by-the-way is Cypriot fire water. It used to be 80% proof, then Cyprus joined the E.U (European Union) and Zivania (along with bird trapping) went to pot!
Today's Zivania is piss water in comparison to the pre-E.U hard-stuff.

Today's Zivania cannot arouse the old boys back in the villages. With Pre-E.U Zivania, the old men could give chase to the Philippineza around the fields, whilst the old lady is having her nap.
Philippineza by the way is a Post-E.U Cypriot term for a lady from the Philippines hired by the now E.U wealthy families of old village folk for domestic duties – which does not include being groped by the old boy.

Apart from drinking, we used Zivania as a cure for all ailments in the old days. If you had a backache or muscle strains, you rubbed Zivania on the sore parts. Any cuts were also treated with the stuff, but it did sting like a bastard.
If your ear hurt after EPS (ear-pop-slap, covered in a previous chapter) you just poured a teaspoon of the stuff in your ear canal and if that didn't work, you'd drink a tablespoon and that would put you to sleep.

So.... gunpowder....
I borrowed some of my brother's birthday money and nipped down the corner shop for as many large boxes of matches four pounds and fifty pence could buy. With the rest of his tenner, I bought some comics, sweets, a couple of cans of Tizer and I still had some money left over for a rainy day.
I have to quickly mention that this was a Saturday at the Pakeman Street house. Older brother was at the restaurant and big sis was at her Saturday hairdressing job.
Mum with younger sis was out most of the day shopping.
Perfect, we had the house to ourselves.

Time to get alchemy with younger brother.

I started cutting all the match heads off and putting them into the professional catering blender that dad had bought mum to help her with all the homemade food for the restaurant she had to prepare. I changed the blade – I removed the blend blade and replaced it to fine cut.

The smart ones amongst you have already guessed what happened, but for the rest of you (not wise to the world of pyrotechnics) I shall continue...

Young brov was itching to do something, but I was moderately responsible for an early-teen and would not let him hold a knife or scissors. He did help scoop up all the five hundred and forty match ends and place them in the blender, but that wasn't enough for him. I told him that when the time comes, he can press the button on the machine. He was satisfied with that.
<Right don't do anything until I come back.> I said.
I went upstairs to the toilet and started emptying a toilet roll from its paper.
I remember pan-icking (excuse the pun).
Oh no, the toilet won't flush. I flushed again. The paper's not going down. Why did I put the whole roll in at once?
On the next flush, I started to see the bottom of the bowl and water again. One more flush should do it......
It was on that final flush that I heard a loud prolonged bang. Bangs by nature are instantaneous...BANG and it's gone. This

one sort of dragged itself out. It was accompanied by a loud fizzing noise and then followed by a scream. My little brother's screams...

I ran downstairs as fast as my skinny legs would manage and jumped off from the fifth step from bottom.
Big brother held the record for jumping off the stairs. He once jumped off from the ninth step - but he has longer legs.
I ran down the hallway and into the kitchen.
I ran into numerous micro infernos. Roughly five hundred and forty of them. Five hundred and forty little fires all over the kitchen. Some all over my brother.
His face was bright red and covered with pockmarks.
The food blender was alight and the plastic lid was lying on the floor, in three pieces.
Where to start? I started slapping my brother's head (mum would have been proud) and managed to get all the flaming match heads off him. As luck would have it, the match ends which had scattered all over the kitchen linoleum floor were extinguishing on their own accord as they burnt out. The problem was, as they burnt out, they left hundreds of pea-sized burnt craters.
The vinyl table cover with the floral pattern smouldered and filled the kitchen with an acrid smell of burnt plastic.
I placed the four-piece condiment set on the floor whilst I folded the vinyl cloth and chucked it out into the garden.
The vinyl was of a decent thickness so the lit match ends did not burn through to the table. Not that it mattered. I later

found out that the floral vinyl table cover cost more than the table.

My brother had stopped crying.
I looked around at the chaos little brother had caused. There was no getting out of this one. There was no excuse I could make up and there was no lie I could tell that would result in me avoiding any form of punishment.
I cleared up all the match ends and swept the floor. I wiped the walls and hid the blender behind some crap in the garden.
I found some old nappy rash cream in the back of the medicine cupboard and told little brov to cover his burns on his face and arms. I thought of bribing little brother to confess to the whole thing. But one look at his sad red tearful streaked burnt face and I felt guilty. No, this was one incident that I will have to take the full blame for. It was time to stand up and face the music. Admit to the offence. Apologise and accept the consequences like a man. Confess the crime – do the time. Cleanse the soul. Take one for the team (my team – me)! Bite the bullet. Pay the piper. (*Almost done*). Look death straight in the eye. Grow some balls......
I heard the front door open.
I went to the door. It was my mum and little sis.
<Can I help you with the bags mum?.... No? Oh ok.....Erm, I'm going out – bye!>

I came home many hours later after hiding out in my cousin's house. I walked into the front room. My mother was there sitting in the armchair reading her Greek magazine. She didn't

look up. Big brother was there with a big smirk on his face. Big sister was there shaking her head. Little brother was there (with red marks on his face) pointing at me as I walked in with a "here he is" expression. Little sister was there looking concerned.
I stood by the television set placed in the corner of the room. I had my hands in my pocket. I looked down to avoid eye contact with big brother and sister and in the most humbling voice I could muster, I said <*I'mm sssorry*!>

The lino floor wasn't replaced for years. A constant reminder to a crazy idea that could have resulted in the house burning down or little brother (and I) suffering a life changing disfigurement.
There was no punishment or beats that day. A lesson learnt for all I guess.

* * *

Christmas day at our house ....and walnuts!

If you thought my stories and escapades were the immature actions of a retard, then within the following tale may be the olive that slips off the donkey's back.
Of all my capers that I have shared with you guys, this is the story that I am most ashamed of.....to a degree.

You can find humour in other people's mishaps, as long as nobody is hurt. Well nobody was hurt in the following tale, but there are limits and boundaries that one cannot cross – well "we" crossed it that day.

After considering the implications of retelling the events, I decided to include it.
Today it is embarrassing and morally unacceptable. Back then, it was also totally deplorable, but the difference is back then, the culprits thought it was unashamedly funny!
Since this is a one off, tell all autobiography, I am obliged to include it
The fitting part is that the poor victim had it coming – well in my eyes anyway.
If I ever get to write a prequel (The Cyprus Years) then this guy will give me enough material for the prequel to have a sequel (More Cyprus Years).
Before I proceed, I must stress and remind you guys that I and the other felons were under the ages of ten. This does not excuse our behaviour, but kids back then were backwards compared to the kids of today.

I also appreciate that I have to be cautious with how I describe the events. It involves what can only be described as inappropriate mono self-sexual contact (I'm struggling for the right terminology here).

This tale takes place one Christmas day.

Twas the day of Christmas, when all through the house, Greek immigrants were stirring.
The children were nestled under the table, bored shitless, so they concocted a plan that involved walnuts and skidmarks!

This incident took place in Pakeman Street – in the first year I think. As you see, I didn't want to include this story in the Pakeman Street chapters for fear of losing the reader at an early stage. We are nearly at the end of the book now and fantastic reviews are sure to follow from those who stuck with it....up until this last chapter where I can be forgiven.

If my parents were not fighting with each other, then they were fighting with my dad's siblings. One Christmas they were on talking terms with each other and with most of the aunts, uncles, *komparous* and *komaires*. This called for a large Christmas gathering.

A quick translation and explanation of the Cypriot words Komparous (masculine) and Komaires feminine).
A Komparo in simple terms is a best man.
Komparous (plural) is best men.
Komaira is one of the maids of honour (Plural Komaires). In Greek Cypriot weddings, the groom has many best men who pay the groom for the privilege. Once a man becomes your Komaparo, that man is bound to you – like an unwanted brother. Also the man who becomes your Komparo has the honorary title of Komparo. For example, a man called Frederick becomes my Komparo (one of my best men). If one day I am at a bar with some work colleagues and Frederick walks in, I will introduce Frederick to my colleagues as Komparo-Frederick. It will be an insult if I introduce him as just Frederick! Also, throughout the night (if Frederick decided to hang around for the next round) I can only call him by his title – Komparo and I must pay for all his drinks!

My colleagues are not allowed to call him Komparo or Komparo-Frederick. He is just Frederick to them.

There is another way someone become your Komparo and that is if he christens one of your kids. Then you have the added edict which is that the Komparo's wife now becomes your Komaira even though she was not one of the maid-of-honours at your wedding. Only a wife of a Komparo who christens your kids can become a Komaira. The wife of one of your best men (Komparo) who has not christened your kid is not a Komaira. There was an incident when somebody called the guy who sold him a donkey a Komparo, but that was frowned upon by the Church and the local Mayor.

Now that's cleared up......

I have only ever experienced one such gathering. It was like the film Highlander – there can only be one, because people tended to lose their festive heads after three bottles of Johnnie Walker Black Label.
The whole room was almost taken up by a combination of tables pushed together, covered with two large tablecloths sewn together on mum's industrial sewing machine. The chairs were pushed under the tables and when the hoard pulled them out to sit on, there was no room at all to move about. This however was not a problem. This wasn't your normal Christmas turkey dinner. This was a Cypriot banquet with all Cypriot dishes made by my mother and aunts laid out for all to help themselves.

There were stuffed vine leaves, Cypriot meatballs, the Greek version of lasagne called Macaronia-do-fonou (with thick tubes of macaroni), jellied pigs trotters, ears and tongues (called Zaladina – my favourite), plenty of olives, mountains of bread, halloumi shipped in from Cyprus, whole raw artichokes, Greek salads, chicken legs, chicken liver and hearts. Cold dips such as tzatziki and tahini. Everyone's favourite kouloumbra (a cross between a cabbage and a turnip – eaten raw with 120 grams of salt). Another favourite was afelia -cubed pieces of fresh coriander marinated with pork (one for the Cypriots out there). I could go on, but I've started to drool.

For the stiff-upper-lip English not drooling whilst reading the above - imagine Yorkshire puds cooked five ways – mmm).

There were no courses. Everything was laid out, including the sweet and nuts. Nuts were vital for lining your stomach before you hit the whiskey. As soon as the first person arrives – the feast begins... and continues when the second and the rest of the family arrive!

Eventually there was no room on the head table for me and my younger cousins – so we were relegated to the kids table which happened to be the floor underneath the head table.
My big brother took great delight in that and when my dad's komparo (see explanation above) poured him a measure of whiskey, I fumed!

I decided I wanted some whiskey too, so I bum-shuffled over to my dad's komparo's end of the table with younger cousins in tow. I had finished my dinner so I carted off the basket of walnuts (and nut cracker) with me and sat beside his legs. I tugged at the komparo's trousers and when he looked down, I asked in my most adoring look I can muster <*Can I have some whiskey please?*>
The Komparo, by that time had finished off one bottle of holy water and was cracking the seal on the second bottle to my father's approval. I tugged again and before I could ask him for

a sip of whiskey, he eyes the walnuts. The Komparo says, <*Pass me some de-shelled walnuts and will think about it.*> But I hear, <*Pass me a de-shelled walnut and I'll pour you a double.*> So with little hands, I place a walnut on the floor and proceed to pummel it with the chrome metallic nut cracker. Eventually the walnut smashes to pieces against the hard linoleum floor. I pick up the bits of nut along with fragments of shell and hold them up to the Komparo.
<*Vre, what is this?*> he says with a slight slur to his voice.

Another pause for translation.
"Vre" is the Greek Cypriot word for "oi"! Actually "Vre" is the masculine for "oi". There is a feminine word which is "Vra"!
The Greek Cypriot dialect comprises of many masculine and feminine words. I think it's called grammatical gender and the Greek Cypriot dialect is packed with them.
My favourite is the gender specific words for "crazy". "Enai Trelos" – He is crazy.
"Enai Treli"- She is crazy.
Anyway, I've digressed. Back to the story..........

<*It's walnuts,*> I say. <*Can I have some whiskey now?*>
<*This is not walnut Vre Ftiri. Don't smash them to bits next time.*>
All I heard was the word "Ftiri" – the Cypriot slang for "fleabag". Needless to say, that pissed me off! I turned to my cousin and his sister who were under the table with me. I told them that he just called us all "fleabags".
It's not the first time this geezer has got on my nerves today. Before he arrived, that was my chair he now has his fat arse on. The thought of getting a sip of whiskey went from my mind. I wanted payback. I looked at the walnuts in my hand. I

looked at my cousin's sister – the bed wetter. I remembered that I hadn't had a bath for two weeks. I remembered that I hadn't changed my underpants in days. I am vaguely aware that I forgot to wipe my arse on the last two or three occasions after number twos, even after my mother embarrassed me in front of my older sister one night at the launderette. My mother held up one of my white underpants (all underpants were white in those days) between her thumb and finger and showed me the brown long stain (a skidmark) and said if I don't wipe my backside properly, she will make me lick them! Big sister then told big brother. They went from calling me Frying-Pan to Shit-Pan. So unnecessary!
I cleared that thought and went back to my devious, most revolting plan to date.

Once again, I humbly apologise for my past actions. I apologise to you, the reader for having to read the following nauseating childish antics, when you could be reading the autobiography of a celebrity who won Celebrity Big Brother. Or the biography of an ex-footballer who slept with his mother-in-law and blew all his money gambling.
Alas, all the heroic, interesting and pragmatic accomplishments in my life happened after I left Holloway. They will be included in the Sequel I will write called "The Finchley Years". Until then Mon'Amie............

I picked another walnut from the basket and this time I carefully broke the shell by placing it within the jaws of the chrome metallic nut cracker and then smacking it on the lino floor. It worked. I ended up with two whole half pieces of walnut. (If you know what I mean).
I kept one half myself and gave the other half to the bed-

wetter. I then instructed her to do what I do.
I undid my trouser button and pulled the zip down. Without exposing myself, I put my hand holding the half walnut down my trousers into my pants and proceeded to rub the nut along the stained seat of my underpants. Only after I imagined grooves in the skidmark, did I pull my hand back out. I gave it a sniff...<*Christos kia Panayia mou.*> Translation – *Christ and Mother of Jesus.*
My cousin, the bed-wetter did not struggle as much. She had a skirt on. When she completed her part and handed me her half of the nut, there was a stink vapour trail like the one in the cartoons starring the French Skunk Pepe-le-Pew.
With eyes watering, I tug at the Komparo's trouser leg and lifted my hand up with both halves of the walnut in my palm. <*Oh bravo, bravo, keep them coming*> he says, pissed as arseholes. He takes a swig of whiskey and tosses the nuts in his mouth. With stifled laughter, my cousins and I shuffle back underneath the table. Only when we reach the centre do we let out a roar of laughter.
<*Again*> I say.
We repeated the cracking of the walnut, the wiping on the skidmark and the dousing in the urine soaked knickers a further three times. The more we laughed the more urine my cousin produced. My Y-fronts were almost clean by the fifth time. It was this that probably gave us away. I had to go one further. Instead of rubbing the walnut on my pants, I went the whole hog and placed it between my dirty arse cheeks.
I remember the Komparo's facial expression. A gagging reflex. He brings the nut up to his mouth. Then to his nose. He gags. He's pissed, but there is a cognitive process still at work. He stares at my face looking up from under the table. The table

cloth around my head gives me that saintly Mother Teresa look. He looks back at the nut and then places it down on the table. <*No more Vre,*> he says with a defeated look.
<*Can I have some whiskey now?*> I smirked.

* * *

The Loulilizer – Another had to be there moment!

My dad came home from work one afternoon – a break between the lunchtime shift and evening shift. My big sister and I were in our bedrooms. Big sis had her Fidelity record player on listening to Tina Charles "I Love To Love". I was planning on playing with my deck of cards.
Dad called us both to come downstairs. After calling up a further three times we finally go downstairs.
Dad gives big sis forty pounds and says <*Go to Rumbelows with your brother and buy a Loulilizer, a good one for the restaurant.*>
I cracked up laughing!
<What's a Loulilizer dad?> Big sis asks.
<*It mixes food and makes sauces,*> dad says.
I crack up again.
I don't know what it is that makes me laugh. I haven't a clue what a Loulilizer is. I know what dad's saying is wrong, but his accent coupled with that word has me in stitches.
<*Tell the man in Rumbelows you want a Loulilizer for a restaurant and he will know.*>
I'm trying to stifle a laugh when dad gives me that look that says, *laugh one more time – I dare you!*

Big sis takes the money and takes me by the scruff and off we set to Rumbelows the electrical retailer.
The distance to Rumbelows, which is on the corner of Hornsey Road and Seven Sisters Road is four hundred and twenty metres from our house. That's roughly one thousand, three hundred feet. At intervals of approximately fifty feet, I stop walking. I make my sister stop walking. I look up and say <*Loulilizer*> and then roll on the pavement laughing whilst holding my belly. At first, she was laughing with me, but after stopping twenty six times and taking twenty five minutes to complete a five minute walk, she too dared me to laugh one more time.
<*Loulilizer!*> Laugh......SMACK!
We get to Rumbelows. My sister and I walk in and we are approached by an Indian guy who is wearing a name badge with the name James written on it.

In the 1970s, foreigners were requested or felt a requirement to give themselves a name appreciated by anglophiles. "Philes"- from the Greek word *Friend.*
I've met many namesakes who changed their name from Panico to Peter.
I've often wondered if my life would be different if I was called Peter at school and not Panico. I am a great believer in the concept "*You Are What You're Named*"! For example, I knew a girl called Fatima and guess what? Yep, she was a large girl. If you call your child Bob, he will grow up to wear a flat-cap. Someone called Bambos will be a bit on the thick side and a butt of Greek Cypriot jokes. Every Stelios I knew was bald by the time they reached the age of twenty five. Most Barrys would be tradesmen and Nigels will work in banking. Trevors

will be train-spotters or model car collectors and Stavros would spend more time in the bookies than at work.
I've never met a Panico I didn't like and I've met Panicos who changed their name to Peter who were right gits!
I like my name. Of all my nicknames I prefer Pan-the-man! (Insert smiley emoji)!

Back at the store...
James (Javinder) smiles a greeting and asks, <*can I help you?*>
<*Do you have any Loulilizers?*> Sis asks...
I couldn't contain myself. I accidently blew out a small snot-bubble through my left nostril and managed to let out a little squeak of a fart out of my arse, as I burst out laughing.
<*A what?*> James enquires, doing a double take at my snot bubble.
<*Please don't say it sis,*> I plead.
<*A Loulilizer. It's for a restaurant. To mix sauces and make food.*>
It's not the word itself. It is the way my dad said it that still resonates in my head. I'm laughing like a hyena when I feel a slap across my head. It has no effect. James looks confused and slightly irritated.
Big sister went apologetically red and smacks me again around the head. She says sorry to James and indicates that she will be right back. She then proceeds to push me out of the store with a slap to the back of my neck for every step I took and for every laugh I coughed out.

I'm outside the store with my face pressed against the shop window looking in. There's an animated conversation going on inside. I tap on the window and when big sis turns to look, I slowly mouth the word <*Lou-Li-Lizer.*>

I thought I saw a smile crack on her face. She turns towards another shop assistant who has joined James and the conversation continues. The new guy goes in the back and a minute later arrives with two boxes. Big sister then points to one of the items and takes the money out of her bag.
I've stopped laughing. I am interested to see what she is purchasing. I open the door and creep in and when she turns towards me, I hold up my hands in surrender and a promise that I'll be good.
<*What is it?*> I ask in all seriousness.
<*It's a bloody liquidiser,*> she says and then we both crack up laughing....

Told you. A had to be there moment!

* * *

Bubbly Bubblegum

A new bubblegum arrived in sweetshops. It revolutionised blowing bubbles. The packaging said you could blow the biggest bubbles ever. It was juicier than other gums and by far the stickiest. One Bubbly Bubblegum could fill your gob and if you put two in your mouth, it would take you forty minutes of jaw-hurting chewing to reach the consistency for blowing bubbles the size of Zeppelins.
There were kids at school blowing bubbles which covered their entire heads chewing only one Bubbly. These gum experts would command an audience during playtime and other kids would encircle the best of them and would applaud at the size of the bubble or the pop of the bubble bursting. For some reason, blowing bubbles didn't come naturally to me.

I struggled with the basics. There was a skill to it which I couldn't master. It could have been my buck-teeth or it could be something as simple as practise makes perfect. But Bubbly Bubblegum cost more than the other gums. Once again, I found myself disadvantaged and unable to achieve a task which even the most unpopular kids could do.

A month after Bubbly came on the market, the school playground was covered in the stuff. Girls' hair was stuck together and boys' trousers always had sticky patches on their bums. You spent ages scraping it off the bottom of your plimsolls and eyebrows if you were skilful enough to blow a bubble which engulfed your head when it burst.
I still couldn't blow a bubble which touched my runny nose.

I needed quantity to practise and perfect this ability.
One afternoon, after primary school finished, I headed straight to Sid's sweetshop. With the money I found in my dad's pockets, I was able to purchase two whole anorak pocket's full. I set off home to practise.
I arrived home and knocked on the door. The door opened and before I could run inside, my mother stepped out with her coat on and closed the door behind her.
<*Come with me to your aunt's house for a minute,*> mum says.
<*Are you talking to her?*> I asked to no reply.

Five minutes later we arrived at my aunt's house. Something serious was going on because my mum and auntie headed straight for the back room. I knew it was serious because my aunt put me in the front room – The Sala!

Another pause for another quick Greek to English translation. The Sala. Or Saloni. The posh living room. The parlour where

Greek Cypriots would receive only their special visitors or doctors. No matter how poor you were, if you had a room that didn't have a fold down bed in it, then you would furnish it with only the best Onyx furniture and ornaments. Immediate family members would never be shown into the Sala. Children were NEVER allowed into the Sala.

No doubt about it, the adults have something really urgent and important to discuss. I'm stood in my auntie's Sala. I stand there in awe. I look around and take it all in.
We didn't have a Sala then, but a year later we did – but it was never this fancy. My aunt's Sala was like something out of the Cypriot magazine House and Donkey. There was a three piece suite covered in transparent plastic sheets stretched tightly over them. There was a green marble (Onyx) coffee table with green Onyx ashtrays at each end. A small green box which I discovered contained mouldy looking cigarettes. Also on the table were two cigarette lighters, again set in Onyx. At either side of the three seater there were tall brass-looking ashtrays. I thought they were gold. Perhaps they were.
It wouldn't be a Greek Cypriot house if it didn't contain at least one lemon geranium. My aunt's Sala had two – the size of me. On the wall was a large painting of a gypsy looking woman with a healthy cleavage. There was a large wooden sideboard and the top of it was covered with a white lace cloth – most likely from the Cypriot village of Lefkara.
On top of the lace were porcelain figurines. There was one of two old men on a bench and another of a woman holding two baskets. There was a Spanish bullfighter and a flamenco dancer.
The one at the back was odd. It wasn't porcelain but plastic and it was of a man with a barrel around his middle. I was

drawn to it. I carefully reached between two figurines and pulled out the plastic figure of the man in the barrel. I carefully examined the piece and noticed that the barrel was not fixed to the man. I tried to pull the barrel down, but it did not move. I held the man by the feet and carefully began to see if it moved up. It did. I held the figure close to my face as I put in slightly more effort to lift the barrel higher over his head. Just then a large penis flicked up from the bottom of the barrel and nearly hit me in the eye. This easily beat the plastic figurine my dad had in his restaurant. It was of a donkey and when you pulled its ears, a cigarette would come out of the donkey's arse.
No, this man in a barrel figure was pure class. I could see why this was placed in the Sala.

After fifteen minutes thorough examination of the Sala, I was getting bored. I put my hands in my pocket and felt the wrappers of Bubbly Bubblegum. I'd forgot all about them. I'd forgot all about my mission to blow the best and largest bubble-gum-bubble. I got chewing!

A newly popular kid in school told me that the art of blowing a big bubble was all in the manipulation of the gum – obviously not in those words. His actual words were ...
<It's the way you chew it and flatten it with your tongue.>
I got to chewing one Bubbly. I was careful not to under-chew and leave bits in, nor over-chew making the gum harden. I chewed just as the flavour started to dissipate but not fade altogether. Then I stopped chewing with my teeth and started to work the gum with my tongue and the roof of my mouth.
I was ready. I pushed the gum towards the top of my front teeth. Then I massaged the gum down to the opening of my mouth, keeping the gum held in place by my teeth. Then I

pushed my tongue in the middle of the gum forcing some out of my slightly opened mouth whilst the rest of the gum was held by puckered lips. I blew. I blew too hard and out popped the gum on the carpet. <*Bollocks.*> I picked the gum up off the carpet. I picked at the stubborn pieces in the carpet too and I got most of them off. I was going to bin the gum in one of those ashtrays but when I looked carefully at it, there was not a dust spec or pubic hair on the gum. A credit to my aunt who kept the Sala spotless. Had it been my house and the gum fell on the lino floor, it would be covered in cat hairs, old Tarzan hairs and bogeys!

I put the gum in my mouth, gave it a quick chew and commenced straight to the blow. The result was an average bubble. Nothing to brag about. As were attempts number three and four. I unwrapped another Bubbly Bubblegum and stuck that in my mouth. A few minutes later, with two gums in my mouth, I got to blowing.

It was no good. I could hardly push the gum out with my mouth. I couldn't make that pocket where the air would fill and inflate. I spat out both gums, put them on the sideboard and opened up a new Bubbly wrapper. Whilst I was chewing, I started to play with the discarded two-gum-lump. I started to stretch it. It stretched and stretched and it never snapped. I stretched the two-gum blob as far as my outstretched arms would go and still it was intact.

EUREKA MOMENT. If I can't beat the record for the biggest bubble, I will create and hold a new record for the longest bubble gum string. Back in my mouth went the two-gums along with gum number three. With dribble running down the sides of my mouth, I got the three gums into one large lump of goo. I then rolled the lump in my licked down palms (to stop the gum sticking) and then I pulled and stretched a bit and pressed it hard onto the sideboard. I then started to stretch out the gum string. Success, I managed to stretch out a gum the entire width of the Sala without it breaking. Could I beat my own record? There was only one way to find out.

I couldn't manage four Bubbly Bubblegums so I chewed four in two shifts. By the time I compiled a four lump dollop, my jaw was ready to drop like Jacob Marley's.

I stretched out the gum the entire length of the Sala but the middle sagged and stuck onto the cigarette case on the coffee table. I wasn't sure if this annulled the world record so I left it in place and set about chewing the last four Bubblys in my pocket. As I struggled with jaw lock, the first gum string across the width of the room also sagged and stuck onto the lace cloth on top of the sideboard. With a record on the brink of collapsing and the other not valid, I started on the third string lost to the world. I placed one end on the window seal and started to stretch. Then it occurred to me that if I twisted the gum string, it would strengthen and............. <*VREEEEEEE.*>

I nearly shit myself. I didn't hear the door open. My aunt is standing by the open door screaming at me. My mother is stood behind her unusually quiet –not angry at all. My aunt shouts out in Greek, <*WHAT THE DEVIL ARE YOU DOING?*> Then she makes the mistake and storms in to closely inspect the mess I've made in her Sala. She's only gone and made things worse by getting tangled in the bubble gum strings. Now the gum is all over her and the floor. <WELL?> my aunt yells.

I'm lost for words. I've gone all sheepish. I creep by my aunt and go towards the sideboard. I reach behind the figurines and pull out the guy in the barrel.

<*Look what auntie has mum,*> I say as I lift the barrel exposing the large penis.

* * *

And Finally - Nunchucks

The school in Holloway for boys had an after school cinema club. Attendance was usually on the low side, until one evening when the organiser decided to show Enter the Dragon. Tickets went on sale for fifty pence on a Monday morning. By Monday afternoon all tickets were sold out. Thursday evening, the hall was packed with boys.

We all heard about the film Enter the Dragon when it was first released in the UK, but none of us at that time had ever seen it. Not for the want of trying though. I tried to sneak in with big brother and his friends, but they slung me out. Seeing people come out of the cinema after watching Enter the Dragon was a spectacle. You would see pairs of boys or men exit the cinema and immediately start slow-motion kung-fu fighting and you would hear screams of Whaaaaaaai!
My big brother and his mates went one better and had a group kung-fu fight. My brother stood in the middle of a cycle made up of his mates and they charged at him – one at a time and in slow motion. More shouts of Whaaaaaaai and Yeeeeeaaaaiiii and my brother would round-house kick, chop and rapid punch them all down. Then he would do that straining thing Bruce Lee did. He clenched his teeth, tensed his arms and

twisted his head round slowly. Similar to pushing out the longest and fattest turd ever.

Now it was my time to see Enter the Dragon. I took my seat along with my friends and laid out some sweets on my lap. The lights went out and on rolled the cine movie projector.

These projectors can be found on eBay in the vintage pages. They heated up the room and made such a racket, that you barely heard Bruce Lee say "Yes Mr Blaithwaite" instead of "Braithwaite"! Also, if the room (or hall) was not pitch-black, you would not be able to tell Bruce Lee and Bolo Yeung apart.
Anyway, I won't dwell on Enter the Dragon. Even though I've memorised most of Bruce Lee's lines...such as (and this isn't me Googling) "Boards don't hit back" and "My shtlye (style) is the art of fighting without fighting". One more..."We need emotional content".

Enter the Dragon was as good as my big brother said it was. And you got to see tits!
We didn't even wait to exit the hall. We started slow-motion kung-fu-ing there and then! We continued to slow-motion fight outside the hall and on the way home down Camden Road and into Holloway Road where my friends and I headed off in different directions, but that didn't stop us shouting, <Whaaaaaaii.>
I arrived home and slow-motion kicked the cat and when my mum turned her back, I slow-motion kicked her just short of any contact on her arse. I avoided slow motion fighting with big brother as that always ended up in normal speed fighting where I would get pinned sown and gobbed at in the face. That night I promised myself that I would learn kung-fu. And learn to be a Nunchunk!

Nunchunk is the word for somebody who has mastered The Nunchuckers – I think. Not to be confused with a fat-nun joke.........

For those who don't know what Nunchuckers are; – They are martial arts weapons. Two hardened sticks held together by a steel chain. You hold one of the sticks and flick the other stick (held by the chain) onto your opponent's head.
You can dazzle and confuse your opponent by twirling the Nunchuckers in front of you and behind your back.
Bruce Lee was able to flick the Nunchuckers over his shoulder and catch the flying end with his other hand and then throw it over the opposite shoulder and again catch it at lightening speeds – and just as his opponent is mesmerised, Bruce would whirl the Nunchuckers around his waist and then smack his adversary in the face or side of the head.

The problem with Nunchuckers was that you couldn't practise in slow motion due to the centrifugal force required to launch the object around one's body. So you dived straight in with Nunchuckers – spinning and snaking the sticks at one hundred Newtons – that's the mass of the Nunchuckers times the velocity...divided by the clunk it makes when it hits the soft spot on top of your head.

On the film's first release in the UK, hundreds of children and adults ended up in Accident and Emergency wards with a variety of head traumas and broken bones. So some clever person started to make them out of plastic and now they are polluting the oceans.

As luck would have it, the following day at school, we had woodwork. There was only one thing my buddies and I wanted to make and that was Nunchuckers. We convinced the woodwork teacher, an ex-carpenter with a chip on his shoulder (pun alert), that we were going to make some draught pieces out of the twenty five millimetre wooden doweling rods. But instead of cutting the each rod into twenty four small pieces, we cut the rods into lengths of a foot. Two times one foot rods for each of us. We then screwed metallic hooks on the ends of the wooden rods. All that was left was for us was to acquire the steel chains. I had an idea where to get them. Actually, it was big brother's idea from when he made his own Nunchuckers.

A few days later, a letter was sent home to parents stating that once again the school was targeted by vandalism. Pupils were suspected and that the school would not tolerate it and would seek to punish those responsible.

The letter also stated that the boys' toilets in the old building had re-opened and that all the Victorian toilet cistern chains had been replaced at some cost to the school.

* * *

A WORD OR TWO FROM THE AUTHOR:-

That's me I guess – the author. Joke!
Thanks for downloading – or even obtaining the paperback version.
I'm going to purchase ten paperback copies, so guess what my family are getting this Christmas...?
For those who know me - I don't think I'll be able to look you in the eyes again.
For those who don't know me – I'm guessing you still don't.

For reasons mentioned in this book, I wrote my story for my children. I wanted to share with them my upbringing and in turn made the decision to share it with complete strangers too. You have read a biography of a person who is not famous nor likely to be unless I sleep with a footballer or post some "selfies" of my hairy backside. Count yourselves lucky.
I'm not a well-educated person, but I get by.
I read a lot of books. The ones I enjoyed the most are fiction from new/first time, self-published authors.
I have read some autobiographies and biographies of famous sports stars, but I found the endings predictable. Inspiring nevertheless, but for a normal person- the unachievable. They won a cup or went on to be knighted. They beat the odds. They shot their girlfriend through a locked toilet door!

You are not left inspired after reading mine – which is not a bad thing. But I'd like to think that I made you laugh. I'd like to think that, in parts you were entertained. But mostly, that you took the trouble to read an autobiography of a nobody.

Thanks again.

* * *

P/S
I don't do social media. Mainly because I'll end up being trolled for my 1960s/1970s views. Or god-forbid, groomed by some old woman with fishnets.
However, during the design of this book's cover, I had trouble deciding which old pictures to include. To solve this problem, those old pics not used on the cover, I have added onto a social media site (I swore I wouldn't have one of these).
I have also uploaded video clips that are associated with certain chapters -
Feel free to visit this site on Facebook.
Search - Sociably Awkward Frying Pan –
You don't have to "friend-request" as I probably wouldn't accept.
I'm useless as a friend anyway!
If you have any comments – you can leave them on Amazon (reviews) – good or bad welcomed. But bad ones may just send me over the edge........ I haven't shoved a walnut up my arse for ages. Do you want that in your conscious?

If you want to critically rip me a new arsehole but Amazon will not allow abuse or certain four letter words – you can email me at panico.antoniou@btinternet.com

If you're from Holloway or you went to one of my schools – again, email me on above with any gossip.

If you were a P.E teacher at my secondary school – I'm surprised you can read!

PPS
Thanks Biz.......

* * *

Fin..............

VZ cm

Printed in Great Britain
by Amazon